Hungry

for

Love

First published in 2016 by Quartet Books Limited
A member of the Namara Group
27 Goodge Street, London W1T 2LD
Copyright © Lucy Beresford 2016
The right of Lucy Beresford to be identified
as the author of this work has been asserted
by her in accordance with the
Copyright Designs and Patents Act, 1988

A catalogue record for this book
is available from the British Library
ISBN 978 0 7043 7409 6
Typeset by Josh Bryson
Printed and bound in Great Britain by
T J International Ltd, Padstow, Cornwall

Hungry for Love

Lucy Beresford

By the same author:

Fiction
Something I'm Not
Invisible Threads

Non-fiction
Happy Relationships: at home, work and play

For Briony Vallis

'Few pleasures are greater than turning out a perfect cake…'
Rose Levy Beranbaum, *The Cake Bible*

Sussex Pond Pudding

'…until the suet crust is cooked to a nutty brown. To serve, invert your cooking basin over a deep dish and gently work the pudding loose. Then cut into the suet crust to reveal the fragrant lemon poached inside, surrounded by golden sugar and buttery juices…'

Wedding cancelled. Jax is striving to achieve an air of calm endeavour. Her thumbs scurry across the keyboard of her mobile phone, while her wrists rest against the steering wheel to offset the slight tremor in her hands. Her car is tucked into a convenient bulge in the narrow lane, a concave hollow of blackberry bush and cow parsley. As she clutches her phone, pinpricks of sweat gather in the creases of her skin. *Wedding cancelled.* She hesitates. Her chewed thumbnail hovers over the green button.

'Press it,' she thinks. Just press it.

The time on the phone reads 07.50. The sun is rising and the sky is cloud free. The perfect day for a wedding, for rose petals to carpet the ground, for bells to ring out over a ropey rendition of 'Widor's Toccata'. A mile away, the catering crew will be arriving shortly. Men will throw white tablecloths up into the air so they billow out like giant meringues. And girls will adjust the centrepiece peonies Jax's mother Majella has chosen—along with the caterer and Jax's dress. Jax can picture it now. Later this morning, Majella will be installed in the marquee's mess, personally supervising every aspect of food preparation. Every aubergine crisp gracing the pâté canapé must sit at just the right angle. Every slice of spinach roulade must be the same width. Every duck breast seared to the same degree

1

of pinkness to match the peonies—Jax pities the poor chef who thinks he's in charge of the wedding breakfast today, the breakfast to celebrate Jax's marriage to Jonty. The joining together in holy matrimony of two apparently perfectly matched people.

A strong image of Jonty and his shredded wheat hair pops into Jax's head. An image of the two of them in restaurants, at parties, on holiday, in bed. She smacks her forehead on the steering wheel. Emotion, she worries, won't do at all. It might make her change her mind. 'And after what he's done, that would be a disaster,' she reminds herself. Not to say demeaning.

And yet suddenly, here she is, with tears and snot streaming down her face, sobbing for the end of something she'd thought precious, even though it has soured. Instinctively she cups her elbows and gives herself a little hug. Her fingers brush the tiny hairs on her forearms. It's what she used to do as a child, steeling herself to force down some foreign culinary concoction of Majella's if she was to be allowed to leave the table.

A sound in the lane behind her makes her glance up. A giant tractor is now inching its way past, its mud-crusted wheels larger than her car. Her fingers in her ears, clods of earth dropping to the ground, she watches as the farm vehicle rumbles away. For a moment she admires its slow, steady progress.

'Come on,' she whispers to herself, 'you can do this.'

Wiping her face dry, she picks up the phone from her lap and focuses back on the text. *Wedding cancelled.* Another wobble wells from within, and she grips the phone.

That first statement—*Wedding cancelled*—is at least crisp and factually correct. If it had been a headline on one

SUSSEX POND PUDDING

of her articles at *Your Day* magazine (slogan: 'Your Day, Every Day'), Mike wouldn't even need to reach for his blue pen. But her chewed thumbnail reproaches her: this is not an article, this is real life. She is cancelling her wedding. Technically hers and Jonty's, but the decision is, scarily, hers alone.

Jax's thumbs flit across the keys again. *Please do not call as trying to work things out.* She hesitates. But she has worked it out. Last weekend for example, before the hen night Caryl had organised—with the tenpin bowling, the tequila shots and the tinselled tiara—Jax had drawn up a list of pros and cons. She hadn't even mentioned the 'con' that Posh Peter had once lunged for her at a party when she was already dating Jonty—an action which had carried with it connotations of being shared around between flatmates like a carton of milk from the fridge. No, the list of cons could have been even longer than they were. Which is why Jax—days later, still picking tinsel out of her hair—is confident that she's doing the right thing.

She smiles as she types the next line: *This is not a joke.* It popped into her head at 4 a.m., just as the dawn chorus began its rural rap. It's designed, she hopes, to stop Posh Peter or any other ushers responding with replies such as 'Phew, now we can watch the Wimbledon final.'

More letters appear on the screen, courtesy of her thumbs. *Apologies to all.* She is thinking, for example, of her bank manager—not that he's been invited—for spending so much money on a dress. And the dressmaker, for wasting her time. And the silkworms, for needlessly consuming copious quantities of mulberry leaves. All for the sake of an ivory Empire line, a modest style sanctioned

3

by Jax's mother, Majella, but paid for by Jax. A sum she can ill afford on what she regularly reminds Mike is a meagre Features Editor salary, but which until very recently she'd assumed would be covered by a joint bank account. She bites her lip. At some point in the next couple of hours she's going to have to apologise to Jonty. Yes, *Apologies to all* must be said.

Which leaves the ending, the final flourish, the signature. Should she sign off as Jacqueline? Or even Jacqueline Mary, as it says on the cream vellum invites? Jx is how Jax always signs off texts and emails. Even to Mopey Mike. Even to her horrid colleague Conrad, who once promised her shoes from one of his celebrity photo shoots but had then 'forgotten', which is ridiculous given that Conrad is so focussed and anal he biros his name on the yoghurts he stores in the office fridge.

So, why should this text be any different? Her thumb deletes the letters until only her initial remains, to which she adds a final '*x*'.

The text is ready to send.

Inside the car her heart is pounding underneath her armpit. Sweat dribbles down the side of her waist and her insides are bubbling like an old jar of Majella's bottled greengages. She opens the car door and swivels in her seat. A light breeze wafts over her newly depilated legs, and she feels a new wave of sadness that Jonty will never again stroke her limbs.

'Which serves him right, the scumbag.' But, God, she misses him. His smile, his fondness for Labradors, the way he shouts at the TV when Ireland lose at rugby. She hates him for hurting her, is appalled—still—at his selfishness, and has spent entire mornings this past week staring blankly at the hole punch on her desk. She misses him with the kind of stretched-out pain which comes from fearing you might never see someone again. She reaches once more for the steering wheel, as if clutching it might steady these alarming recent mood swings.

Eventually she peels her damp palms away from the faux leather. Yes, she's doing the right thing, but is she doing it the right way? Certainly there are no books written on the topic. Who knows: maybe *How to Cancel your Wedding* is the holy grail publishers should be looking for, with its step-by-step chapters, its links at the back to self-help groups and its free CD of Tibetan meditation chants.

But what she really needs is a 'how to guide' to love. She loved Jonty but he smashed her world to pieces. How will she ever be able to trust in love again? If only there was a recipe for love.

She catches herself smiling in the rear-view mirror. Who knows, perhaps her mother knows of a recipe for love. After all, Majella is and always has been a woman in pursuit of culinary perfection. It's a grail Majella believes she can reach next week with the glossy, twenty-fifth anniversary reissue of her hardback bestseller, *Food of Love*, the famous recipe book that once changed the way the nation thought about eating.

But the two Jaxes smile at each other, knowingly. Majella behaving selflessly? The very idea. No, Jax won't be seeking her mother's advice about any recipe for love.

Jax takes a deep breath, and wills her hands to stop shaking. The time has come. She takes no pleasure in what she's about to do, but it is necessary—which is how Majella speaks of greasing cake tins. She reads the text one final time, and then presses the green button. Her phone makes a tiny beep, an audible wink of complicity. A little envelope flutters around the screen; the infamously dodgy phone reception in this part of Sussex might fatally scupper her plans.

But there it goes, the brave little icon, spinning into the ether, taking with it the two dozen most important words of Jax's life so far. The sun is rising now, spreading its benevolent warmth out over the dry earth. The future has begun. She hugs herself again and strokes the delicate hairs on her arms. Despite the sultry temperature in the car, Jax is unsettled to feel the presence of goosebumps.

COFFEE

'…and is sourced from many countries around the world. Bitter in flavor, coffee can be used to enhance sweet dishes, where it goes well with nuts, or as in the following recipe, to add an exotic touch to a deep-coloured sauce which goes particularly well with dark meats…'

Majella is making coffee. Not in the inattentive, bleary-eyed way most people do, but with a commitment Majella believes respects the beans and the farmers who grew them and the brave ancient culture which first thought about smashing them to dust, drowning the powder in boiling water and leaving the slop to stagnate before drinking. Food is nourishment, it is a lyrical metaphor for love. It is also the source of Majella's national fame and comfortable domestic circumstances.

Standing at the kitchen window, sipping the bitter liquid, Majella surveys the marquee and the garden. A wedding. An event happening on her turf for which she has the starring role. My day. I'm in charge.

The only thing she isn't in charge of, she likes to say, 'is the weather'. And even that, she adds, is being taken care of by Desmond, Jacqueline's father, gazing down on them all from on high. And Desmond knows better than to contradict his wife. Which is why it is said, in some circles, that Majella killed him, as effectively as if she'd injected cyanide into an apple. Had, the story goes, Desmond been a man confident of his own mind and tongue he would—that fateful day back in 2004, at that dinner held to celebrate the Portuguese imprint of Majella's bestseller *Dinners in a*

HUNGRY FOR LOVE

Dash—have had the nerve, the self-preservation, to whisper 'Majella darling, I think my hake might be off'. And since Majella had catered singlehandedly for the event, using, naturally, recipes from *Dinners in a Dash*, he would have been criticising her cooking, or at least her sourcing skills. Thirty-six hours in intensive care later, and Desmond was no more. Which freed Majella up to be squired tearfully by her agent around TV studios to urge fishmongers and supermarkets to come clean about the turnover time of fish stocks, which led to raucous tabloid backing and a short-lived government-led campaign to *Save Our Soles*.

But whiffy fish is pretty easy to spot, when you're in the know and handle food for a living. So, did Majella know the hake was off, and get rid of her husband? Or did she *not* know, which for a chef is possibly more unforgiveable? The newspapers at the time, asking both questions, came up with answers by inference. Majella went to ground and, three months later, came up with a book entitled *Cooking at My Wake: recipes for the grieving*.

Caryl's in the kitchen too, although she's just a slip of a thing. Ignoring coffee, the breakfast she assembles is bacon and eggs, two chocolate chip muffins and toast with butter and home-made three fruit marmalade. At the table she watches her mother staring out the window, and instinctively pulls her dressing gown round her as if in preparation for a storm. Watches as wisps of steam from Majella's espresso cup tango towards the ceiling.

If only life were as simple as drinking coffee and staring out of windows. Being a daughter, Caryl has decided, is a weird thing. She feels grown-up everywhere but in this house. Majella's aura is like a military defence shield, so that all one's strength—the strength for example required to hold down a job as an inner-city GP whilst fantasizing about being a novelist—is sapped by the kind of maternal glance that hints at ridicule.

At least Majella looks the part, maternal in shape if not temperament, with fabulous breasts the size of a pair of organic chickens. The flesh is similarly puckered and pale but a succulent sight for some eyes nevertheless. She is the mother, the provider of nourishment, together with all the love and nurturing that this implies. And as proof of this, she is a celebrated television chef, doyenne of the daube, the maternal-looking woman who twenty-five years ago, introduced Swiss chard to a grateful nation. Majella shows, at least on screen, that feeding people is a moral good, a selfless act of faith that transcends all other virtues.

But from inside the family, what happens when those myths fail to ring true? When they exist separately, like oil and vinegar in the same bottle? In her central London practice, Caryl treats women battered by their husbands, timidly lifting their burkas to show bruises as big as muffins. In their bony fists they clutch the prescription for linctus to treat the fictitious cough they have used as a cover to attend the clinic. Caryl knows that nothing will change for these women so long as they collude with their husbands that abuse is acceptable.

It is why Caryl admires Jax for the decision she has made. Earlier this morning, from behind her bedroom curtain, she watched as her sister tiptoed along the drive to her car, Jax's wayward blonde hair bouncing perkily with each step. A minute later and Caryl was creeping along the gravel herself. Jax had turned and Caryl had seen—with a smidgeon of envy—that her sister's hazel eyes were newly alive with warmth and possibilities. And although the tip of Jax's nose was flushed pink, suggesting a few recent if understandable tears, her smile was wide and her skin was fresh and glowing as if she was approaching the finishing line of a challenging race.

'God, I'm nervous,' Jax had whispered, grabbing her sister's hand and pulling a face.

No, you're really brave, thought Caryl, turning the hand-holding into a fierce hug.

Caryl puts the empty plates and dirty cutlery in the dishwasher, the butter back in the fridge, the marmalade in the larder and the muffin case in the bin. She is stalling for time. Majella has insisted that, today of all days, the kitchen must be tidy, in case people peek inside to check out the great chef's culinary kingdom. Clean surfaces are Majella's creed. So famous is she for *wiping down* that for several months she appeared on commercial television in an advert for kitchen towels, which upset the BBC greatly. Majella's stands for order, precision and tight-arsed portion control. Nigel Slater and Nigella embody the enemy. For years, Caryl has secretly lusted over the photos in Nigel and Nigella's cookbooks showing batter-crusted spoons allowed to rest on worktops. They suggest to Caryl not just second helpings, but a way of cooking—maybe even of living— that verges on the compellingly sluttish.

Majella, on the other hand, is a control freak. (It has taken Caryl three years of therapy to say this about her own mother; a phrase which has yet to be uttered outside the confidential confines of her therapist's candle-lit basement, where the seat with its Indian throw is always strangely warm from the previous client). Which makes Majella's reaction to the news Caryl is already late in conveying—that the wedding is off—easy to predict.

Which might explain why, before she has a chance to say her sibling-scripted lines, Caryl can feel another visit to the bathroom coming on.

IRON RATIONS

'...and I mean this as a little joke, because of course the phrase refers to the emergency food eaten by soldiers in the field. Food for our brave military, reinforced with vitamins and nutrients, inspires my delicious and healthy pie of Swiss chard and Emmental cheese which...'

Dan is out for an early morning run. Such loose-limbed activity became the norm for him when stationed in Helmand and now in London he hasn't lost the hunger for those feel-good endorphins sloshing around his system. Pounding the desirable stuccoed streets in unfashionably tatty trainers, he quickly enters what athletes call 'the zone'. Sometimes the zone soothes him; right now, it's creating unwelcome space for a flashback. Today's flashback is what shrinks would call the trigger, the crack and flash of the suicide bomber and Gunner Bill on his back, his face on fire.

Dan steps up the pace, to shake off feelings of helplessness. He checks his watch. Jax is getting married in seven hours. Time for one more punishing circuit of this neighbourhood and then he'll take a quick shower at home before opening up. Today of all days, he must keep busy.

He turns the corner and almost runs slap bang into a group of youths in hoodies. As he does so, he is dimly aware of having heard raised voices seconds before. Mid-stride he is about to apologise and body swerve his way back into his run when he notices the pile of clothes on the ground, filthy clothes, and a raised foot kicking the clothes, kick followed by kick, accompanied by jeers. All this Dan un-

12

derstands in the blink of an eye, summing up situations according to the army mantra: 'the absence of the normal and the presence of the abnormal means it's suspicious; if it's suspicious, it stays suspicious until normality returns'.

'Oi, clear off,' he bellows, roughly shoving the kicker away.

The lads are young, stringy, cocky. They make to square up to him but, despite their numbers, can instantly tell that against Dan—six foot one and steady in demeanour—they stand not a chance. They sprint away.

Dan crouches down beside the pile of clothes. Something within them lies in a foetal position, while old hands cupped like a badger's paws cradle a head of matted hair. The stench makes Dan want to gag. 'It's OK. They've gone.' He forces himself to keep a hand on what might be a shoulder. Male? Female? It's impossible to tell.

Slowly, limbs take shape, as a body turns. Eventually beneath the hair a craggy face appears. If this was Afghanistan, Dan would now ask where this person lived. But he knows the answer to that one already. The man lives here, as in, on the streets.

He helps the man to a sitting position. His clothes—rags really—are greasy. The man tries to speak but just coughs. Dan is almost knocked back by chronic bad breath. Who knows when this man last ate?

'Come on fella. Come with me. My place is just round the corner.' Dan realises he himself must stink of sweat but at least he can always have a shower back home later tonight.

Slowly Dan walks the old man the half block to Dan's premises. He pops next door to the 24-hour deli to get his spare set of keys and opens up. Switching on the lights, the bare brick/poured concrete interior warms up. He eases the old man onto a stool and heads to the kitchen to put a pan of milk on to simmer.

While a vegetable tart bakes, Dan lifts with ease the remaining thirty or so wooden stools upturned on zinc tables. He grinds coffee beans, throws ingredients into the mixer, pours batter into cases and slides muffin tins into the ovens. Noticing that one of the room's naked bulbs has popped, he finds a functioning one in the stockroom and twists it back into place. And seeing that one of the distressed dressers has been knocked, with a couple of heaves he moves it back against the wall, the grey cotton of his T-shirt taut against his muscles.

Once the old man has drunk his milk and tucked into a plate of baked goods, it's clear he doesn't want to hang about. Dan has seen it before, in people whose homes were destroyed. They would sooner be back in the rubble, rebuilding their lives from what they know, than rehoused in prefabricated centres. He says goodbye to the man at the door and watches him shuffle off. Then he flips the door sign to 'Open'. The Barracks Bakery is now ready to begin another day.

He sneaks one last look at his watch. In six hours time, Jax will be getting married.

TOMATO FOOL

'...especially in the summer months, when tomatoes are at their most refreshing. Peel and deseed a kilo of tomatoes, then puree. Add a spritz of lemon juice. Whip double cream to stiff peaks and fold into the puree. Add caster sugar to taste, and then pour the mixture into chilled glasses for an attractive yet unusual dessert.'

Through the lanes at speed now. Jax turns on the radio. The reception is so scratchy, she's forced to settle for a local station. Punctuating the easy listening tracks, its DJ maintains a running joke about the song lyrics 'you say tomato, I say tomato, let's call the whole thing off'. You say cream, I say magnolia: let's call the whole thing off-white.

All is going well, when a random song request, for Elsie's ninetieth, let's hear it for Elsie, brings up the first few bars to 'Everything I Do, I Do It For You'. A Pavlovian response to this, the song chosen for her First Dance with Jonty, has hot tears streaming down Jax's face once more, although something brave and spirited in her also has her singing along word-perfectly to the lyrics.

With each mile, Jax feels as though she's wading through treacle, struggling to pull away from her old future, with its emerald surrounded by diamonds, its barefoot chic honeymoon in the Maldives, its three children at private school and now bloody Bryan Adams. As she was creeping out of Majella's house, Jax had passed a photo—the sight of it had quite winded her—of her and Jonty in Richmond Park.

Jax slams her foot down on the accelerator. She hasn't seen Jonty in person since the wedding rehearsal, held on the Thursday because Jonty had to dash back to London to sign a heads of agreement. Apparently a document scanned and sent by email wouldn't do. But with the Richmond photo and now the ballad, it's as if he is suddenly in the car—she can almost feel the heat of him, pressing against her body. By cancelling her wedding, she was attempting to airbrush him out of her life. And now she can't get him out of her head. Her stomach does a little shimmy. Which is exactly how she felt when she first met him.

It was at a wedding—which is tidy, given that their relationship is ending at one, too. Conrad and Jax were covering a reader's nuptials. Mike is so antisocial he refuses to attend such events. Which left Jax alone with Conrad who made catty comments about everything—the lupines, the vol-au-vents, the organist in head-to-toe leopard print—as he peered through various lenses. Jax, who loves lupines, loves the way each separate flower can be made to pop open like the mouths of goldfish, attempted to blot out Conrad's monologue and make notes for her copy.

'Why don't women go on diets before they get married?'

'Conrad, have you ever said anything nice about anyone?'

'Shut up, Jax. And move back. You're in my light.'

'No, I think you'll find that's your ego, blocking out the sun.'

At *Your Day*, they are proud that *our photographs complement our prose*. They obviously haven't seen Conrad and Jax working together.

Jonty was a 'work guest', someone known to only half the bridal couple, and therefore whose emotional attachment to the day was diluted. Jax was having trouble doing justice to the Bo Peep theme (sheep rather than bridesmaids) when a vision emerged from the glare of sunshine and sauntered across the lawn. His right hand was slipped casually into one pocket of his striped morning suit trousers, and he nodded to people as he passed as though giving strangers his approval. When he was close enough for Jax to see the dimple on his chin, he nodded at her notebook.

'Making notes for your own wedding?'

'Oh, I'm never getting married,' Jax said, brushing absently at the tiny hairs on her arms. She had decided on spinsterhood ever since walking in on Majella throwing a copper saucepan at Desmond when he had failed to take something out of the freezer as instructed. The idea of marrying someone only to treat them as your sous-chef held no appeal.

But Jonty looked delicious, with the gym-fit build that Jax likes and that streak of the Oirish blarney charm— from his father's side, Jax later discovered—with its hints of ample families and raucous wakes. His constant gaze on her felt unusual, and so perhaps it was this that compelled her to throw down the challenge, this lupine-embroidered gauntlet: find me, chase me, put some effort in. Pay me some attention, in a way my mother rarely does.

Especially as Jonty's reply had been well, 'we'll see about that then'. A reply just the right side of cockiness, delivered with a disarming smile. It was either this exchange, or the two dozen roses he sent the following Monday to the offices of *Your Day* which had clinched it. Previous boyfriends had shied away from such public displays of affection. For days she was bursting with animal energy, feeling properly wanted. Certainly no one had ever couriered flowers to Jax before. 'Everything I Do, I Do It For You'.

HUNGRY FOR LOVE

'You're the icing on the cake', Jonty used to tell her. And Jax could feel her insides melt to feel so adored, so noticed. Only, now, she understands that all along she'd been regarded merely as decoration, like silver balls on icing. That just as Jax had been happy to wear a ring on her finger, so Jonty had wanted to have someone, maybe anyone, on his arm.

At the approach to the South Downs, Jax slows to a crawl behind another tractor. Wiping her eyes with a finger, she reaches in her bag for a tissue resting on her mobile, and immediately sees the problem. Ominously, the question 'Retry?' fills the screen. More significantly, the number of bars down its side is zero. She has no reception. She thumps the steering wheel. The texts haven't even been sent. No one knows Jax has cancelled her wedding. Which is as good as saying, *it's still going ahead.*

With one eye on the tractor in front, her hand shakes as she retrieves the text. For a split second she remembers the Richmond photo and wonders whether she's being given a second chance. To become a wife, Jonty's wife, mother to Jonty's children, lifelong hugger of a man whose training sweat once plastered his T-shirt to his broad chest. The T-shirt Jax washed and ironed innumerable times—without thanks! No, surely she's being given a second chance to be decisive, to maintain her self-respect, to confirm her choice.

Now, as Majella would say, to camera: here's a text I made earlier.

Jax presses the green button. Once more the envelope icon dances across the screen. It spins and spins, for what seems like ages. Jax feels she is about to explode. Up ahead, the tractor is turning, more slowly than city dwellers would imagine is possible in this age of bullet trains and broadband.

C'mon. She must get past the Downs for the reception to improve.

Once the tractor is safely in its field, she slams her foot down on the accelerator again and roars away, over the brow of a hill and out towards Surrey, and London, and her future.

Eventually the phone makes a smug little beep. The texts have finally been sent.

As the local station starts to crackle and break-up, she can imagine the DJ squeaking, beyond excited: and now lucky listeners we have time for one final request, so let's hear it for Jax and Jonty, it's 'Let's Call The Whole Thing Off'.

BLUEBERRY MUFFINS

'…very easy to make. That's because unlike many other cakes, the batter for these does not need to be smooth or well beaten—in fact the less you work on this batter the better! Try these for…'

Standing behind the counter, Dan strokes its smooth oak. The waitress Sonya stands beside the till, replenishing an almost indecent display of blueberry muffins. Sonya's the kind of woman who thinks dangly earrings make up for poor self-esteem. Today she wears ones in the shape of balloon whisks.

The early birds trickle in, sweating in lycra or carrying the Saturday *FT*. My lady, or my gentleman, is how Dan speaks of his clients, his 'guests': can you bring over another seat for my lady, he might say. None of this frenzied *to go* business of global coffee chains here. Despite the exposed-brick walls, the reclaimed zinc tabletops and on tap Wi-Fi, Dan's cafe has cosseting in its DNA.

Dan slices into fresh banana bread. He always had a steady hand, as Brigadier Winters-King was at pains to point out two years ago at Dan's leaving party. Scrupulous attention to manual tasks is, for Dan, an art, a religion. And slicing is no exception.

The loaf yields to his pressure on the blade. He once spent an entire afternoon explaining to Jax—who'd come to interview him for a feature on wedding cakes—about the texture of cakes, known as its crumb. And the various pressures you can use: how fruit cakes respond well to vigorous cutting, but how sponges require the utmost tenderness. And how the knife handle must be of carved

BLUEBERRY MUFFINS

wood to allow for the perfect non-slip purchase. Dan trusts in the mystical properties of baking just as once he trusted in his training to keep people safe. He smiles to think back to that afternoon, how he'd assumed that Jax—given her parentage—was as obsessed with cooking as he was. 'I burn toast,' had been her crisp reply, before asking him another question.

When he's sliced the banana bread, Dan nods reverently at his customer as if passing benediction. He almost doesn't notice the money she's placed on the counter. When he finally registers the vulgar pile of coins, he is embarrassed: as if money sullies the moment, the very idea of baking. With a smile he pushes them back to this regular lady, a war widow, and gently closes his hand over hers. Home-made cakes, Dan feels, ought to be free at the point of delivery: like the NHS, only more beneficial to one's overall wellbeing.

Dan casts his eye around his Barracks Bakery. Every table is occupied—sunny Saturday mornings are excellent for business—Sonya has folded enough khaki napkins to last the weekend, and the new line of strawberry cheesecake slices are selling well.

And yet.

And yet, Dan can feel the sense of helplessness he felt during his run returning. Today, Jax will not be lighting up the premises with her presence.

He checks his watch. Nine o'clock. In around six hours time Jax will be a married woman. He wasn't invited—he and Jax don't know each other that well—but Dan knows all about the wedding. If Jax had had her way, or rather if Majella hadn't stuck her spatula in where it wasn't needed,

21

the Barracks Bakery would have created the wedding cake with matching miniature muffin favours. After several discussions and a few tastings, Jax had settled in her mind on a magnificent pyramid of all the cupcakes in his cafe's repertoire, a cascade of buttercream topped with silver balls for added self-consciously ironic bling.

Dan runs his fingertips along the grain of the oak counter. It's carved from a tree in his parents' garden in Sussex. Dan's father's coffin was similarly sourced. After he'd left the army, and had bought the premises for the bakery, Dan was keen to show his mother the uplifting uses the wood could be put to, feeling this counter take shape under his hands. Absently he feels beneath his skin the ridges of a familiar whorl near the till. He doesn't know what else to do, to blot out the nagging suspicion that once she's married, he might never see Jax again.

Spaghetti alla Puttanesca

'…where it's known as 'whore's pasta.' The sauce of chopped tomatoes, garlic, and black olives is gutsy and colourful, with the added saltiness of chopped anchovies. Although it's usually teamed with spaghetti, this sauce is happy to be paired with any kind of pasta.'

Miranda wakes up in her town house. The sun is just detectable behind damask curtains. Belgravia is so heavenly at weekends.

Miranda doesn't really do the country. When she's more than five miles from Harvey Nichols, she starts to get twitchy. Anywhere outside the M25 and Miranda has been known to hyperventilate. She will accept your invitation to come and stay for the weekend, but only once her secretary's discreet enquiries have ascertained that your children are away at Brownie camp, that there are smart boutiques local to your cottage, and that she can arrive in time for Saturday supper and leave just as the church bells are beckoning the faithful on Sunday morning.

Miranda stretches her legs until her foot finds another warm limb. She strokes it and in response, an arm emerges from the duvet and a melon of a bicep flops across her chest. She feels calmed. A whole weekend in London. She turns onto her side to face him, and ruffles his hair. He grins, but doesn't open his eyes. She plants a noisy kiss on his forehead.

And then she remembers. She doesn't have a whole weekend ahead in London, because she's got to be in wretched Sussex for a wretched wedding. What a perfectly vile way to ruin a lovely morning.

HUNGRY FOR LOVE

She turns to face the window and tugs the duvet sharply around her shoulders. She thinks about calling in sick. She has done that for numerous rustic weddings in the past. Who cares about an empty place at the table? She never eats anything; or not in front of other people, anyway. Or maybe she could say she got stuck in Wimbledon traffic? But that would just mean she'd be late, not a no-show. A last minute work crisis? That's not what the last twelve years has been about, slaving away to become the bank's youngest director. Lately Miranda has taken pleasure in ignoring letters from her old school, inviting her to talk to the girls about 'being a success in the City'. Let Miss Harris—she of the patent black pumps and Bible quotes—look me in the eye now and say that Miranda will never amount to anything.

So she must call in sick. She lifts up the goose-down duvet as a prelude to sliding out of bed. A hand grabs her waist.

'Hey, where are you going?' The voice is drowsily carnal. An Irish whiskey of a voice. It's a great pity, thinks Miranda, that they can't go to this ghastly wedding together.

'Just getting my phone.'

'Come back to bed.'

'I'll be really quick,' she says, sprinting across the polished floorboards.

'Hurry, or I'll have to think of ways to punish you.'

Miranda grabs her phone from her handbag and with a thumbnail tries to switch it on whilst bouncing back into bed. He wrestles her for it, before hoisting himself up and straddling her. The phone emits its familiar 'waking up' jingle.

'Put the phone down or I'll have to put you across my knee.'

SPAGHETTI ALLA PUTTANESCA

'You wish.'

But in one practised movement he places the phone on the bedside table, opens a drawer and removes a short strip of condoms. Then he reaches a toned arm behind her back, lifts Miranda up, and places her further down the bed, at just the right position.

Miranda's phone beeps. She can't help herself, but even with certain eyewatering muscles in front of her, she twists her head in its direction. He strokes her nose with the strip of condoms.

She pouts. 'I've got a text,' she says.

'Yes, but I've got one of these,' he says, reaching into his boxers.

Miranda returns his smirk. He really is looking pretty amazing today. 'Well, I guess there's no contest,' she says, arching her back, looping her arms around his neck, and planting a kiss on his dimple.

CARROT SHORTBREAD

'…and useful to have in your repertoire as it can be made at very short notice. Grated carrot adds interest and texture to the tray bake, but essentially this is still a traditional, unleavened biscuit with a high percentage of butter fat, hence the name…'

The first text Jax receives is from an old school friend, Beverley: *Cant believe youve been dumped poor you bx*

Beverley is not known as Bitchy Bev for nothing. No surprise that she's the first to reply. She'll have been up for hours, trying out various outfits. Upstaging the bride is one of Bev's specialities. Marriage to a hedge fund manager has only increased Bev's sense of entitlement.

Jax is queuing to pull onto a roundabout to get on to the A3 when she receives an awkward reply from Conrad: *Dear Jacqueline, I hadn't realized I'd been invited to your wedding. Consequently, I'm not sure why you think I'd be interested in your latest message. Yours, Conrad.*

His confusion is understandable. Jax believes you should only invite colleagues you actually *like*. And although she did originally place Conrad on the C-list for when people declined, luckily it never came to that. Because seriously, why on earth would she even consider inviting someone to the wedding who uses proper punctuation in texts?

By the time Jax reaches the part of the A3 that meets the M25, a not untypical comment has winged its way from Mike: *You think YOU'RE having a bad day…*

Jax attaches her Bluetooth. Needless to say, Mike— given his publicly acknowledged aversion to the genre— had already declined the engraved stiffie, and was therefore

26

never intending to sit down to spinach roulade sliced to the perfect thickness. But she had included him in on the cancellation text this morning to forestall any gloating when she appears at work on Monday, when Mike—and everyone else—will be expecting her to be sunbathing in a bikini on some tropical atoll.

He answers her call. 'I've always said weddings are bollocks,' he says. She can hear him taking a drag on a cigarette. 'And now you've seen the light. What do you want me to do? Congratulate you both?'

'Well, actually it's just me on this one.'

Mike takes another long drag. '*You've* called it off?'

He sounds incredulous. It's as if Jax has just told him she can get front pew seats for the next royal betrothal. And he almost chuckles. At least Jax assumes it's a chuckle, but it could be smoker's cough. 'So, what are you going to do now?'

This is a very sensible question, and one Jax hasn't given any thought to. Clearly she now has time on her hands, having originally planned to be doing something else this weekend. Or indeed, with her entire life.

She might wash her hair—genuinely. Caryl was going to play hairdresser for the day, and flatten her sister's wurzle frizz. As if in sympathy, Jax's scalp starts itching.

'Well, you know where I am,' concludes Mike, mournfully, as if to say 'I never get to do anything as exciting with my life as cancel a wedding'. Or maybe he just means 'I'll be in Battersea, if you're passing through'. Jax knows Mike's flat. She went there once to drop off some late copy when the computer system had crashed. There were gin bottles in a recycling bag on the landing, and a bow window which leers at the wine bars opposite.

HUNGRY FOR LOVE

Jax says thanks, and rings off. She decides to leave her next encounter with Mike until Monday morning.

So far, these are the only replies. No one has texted to sympathize or offer support. More significantly, Jonty has not rung. Which could mean he and all his ushers are hungover. Or it could mean…? She tries to think what his silence might mean. The lack of response from the majority of guests could have something to do with the bit in her text which said *pls do not call as trying to work things out*. And as Jax is always telling *Your Day* readers in features on Invitation Etiquette, guests love explicit instructions. It makes them feel secure and looked after. And guests who feel secure and looked after will behave themselves on the day and say heart-warming things in their handwritten thank you notes.

But Jonty will go ballistic. Jonty always did have a short temper and Jax can just imagine how he will react to this latest unscheduled development, this public humiliation. She has cancelled their wedding, and the decision is final, but Jonty is Jonty: the money, the temper, the condescending nodding, have all over time affected Jax deeply. Jonty will always be the one with the power.

CRÈME ANGLAISE

'…and some people refer to it as a thin version of the English custard. In most cases it is used as a pouring sauce for desserts but real fans are happy to eat it on its own. If the mixture is frozen, the custard becomes the base for some ice creams…'

Jax walks down the steps to her basement flat. Three pigeons watch her. They are not a popular species in London—they are known as flying rodents—but Jax is fond of this trio and their jerky line-dance routines along her windowsill. Today their necks glisten with pearlescent greens and mauves. Their familiar presence is reassuring, which she hopes will hasten her entry into a state of calm, of certainty. The phone call to Jonty will be the hardest of her life. She has debated the possibility of going round, talking face to face, but today does not seem to be the day for doing things in the flesh. She's looking forward to it about as much as when Mike utters his favourite words: 'I want you and Conrad to…' But surely a call to a soon-to-be ex-fiancé could never be *that* bad.

As soon as she puts the key in the lock, she senses the presence of someone in her flat. Definite sounds emanate from the kitchen along the hall, the jangle of cutlery, of a drawer being opened and closed. And although it is bad luck for bride and groom to meet before the ceremony, part of her is touched that Jonty has chosen to spend his last night of singledom in her bed. The idea of him sniffing her linen brings a smile to her face.

And then she remembers that the wedding is off and that for a reason she doesn't want to think about, she never wants to see Jonty ever again.

HUNGRY FOR LOVE

Feeling clammy, she stands in the hall, stroking the hairs on her arms, wondering how to avoid her now ex-fiancé. She contemplates squeezing into one of the built-in cupboards lining the hall. Jonty, she sees now, intimidates her. By cancelling their wedding Jax feels she's putting herself not in a position of strength and renewal, but of isolation, excluded from life's feasts.

On the floor of the hall lie piles of *Your Day*. The top copy is a Christmas issue, trumpeting an article by Jax on how to cope with interfering in-laws. Set your boundaries and stick to them. It's all a matter of self-confidence.

Jax squeezes her fists tightly together and faces the kitchen.

Which is where she finds Angus, her estate agent. Jax had intended to move into Jonty's flat which is just minutes from the Barracks Bakery, minutes from weekly supplies of chocolate velvet cupcakes, from a lifetime of blissful weekends licking buttercream off sponge. For someone who cannot cook, but who lives for the days of the week when flapjack is the tray bake of the day, the proximity of this culinary haven to Jonty's spacious apartment was heavenly. Jax feels quite weak at the thought that, as well as waving goodbye to Jonty's bratwurst sausage cock and south-facing roof terrace, she is forsaking the Barracks Bakery.

'Jax,' says Angus, shaking hands vigorously. 'I thought you said you wouldn't be home today?' Today's cufflinks are sharks' heads.

She can tell from the way his eyes bore into hers that he is desperately trying to remember what her plans were this weekend, plans which meant he could show someone round the pristine kitchen. And it's not just extravagant

CRÈME ANGLAISE

estate agent speak to say it's pristine, given that Jax struggles to make Cup-a-Soup. Caryl's therapist—she of the dimly-lit room and ethnic fabrics—says it's all part of the girls' resistance to Majella's fixation on food. Majella, even ignoring the psychobabble, is perpetually appalled. 'If you can read, you can cook,' is her mantra, a slogan printed on gold circles and stuck on millions of cookbook dust-jackets. It suggests that Majella, too, regards Jax's inability to make toast as wilful rebellion.

'You've got a lovely flat,' says the woman with Angus. Her hair is the colour of crème anglaise, a straight column created by someone pouring a secret, never-ending supply. 'In fact,' she adds, 'I'm putting in an offer.'

Jax's heart sinks. The reality of my life is this: not only have I yanked out the Barracks Bakery drip, but I'm about to be rendered homeless. 'It's no longer for sale.'

'No!' The woman's cry to Jax's ears is like a wounded fawn. 'But this is awful. Your flat is so darling. I've seen it three times already, although I think I fell in love at first sight.'

Ah, Jax wants to say. Beware of falling in love at first sight. I did, and look what happened to me. 'The thing is, I need my flat back.'

Angus's eyes narrow. 'Weren't you–' He stops himself. His nose wrinkles, and Jax can see his eureka moment. He has finally remembered what Jax was supposed to be doing today.

'Weren't you–' He stops himself again. Having just worked it out, he is clearly grappling with the fear that before him stands a woman newly jilted and therefore presumably on the verge of a nervous breakdown.

31

HUNGRY FOR LOVE

'My circumstances have changed,' Jax manages to say, tightly. 'The flat's no longer on the market. I'm sorry.'

Their eyes meet and, in each other's pallor, they see the tint of dashed dreams. They both understand the other's pain.

Angus escorts a weeping Emily up on to the street while Jax gazes out at her tiny back patio. Pot plants wave optimistically at the source of nutrients, while a neighbour's cat treats the space as a feline tanning salon. Five more minutes, she keeps telling herself. Five more minutes and then I'll ring Jonty.

PISSALADIÈRE

'…mainly from the South of France, in Provence. Each home will have family variations, but in essence this is a rich onion tart, decorated with black olives and anchovies in a variety of designs and patterns. This is a good picnic dish or one to add drama to the buffet table…'

'Your sister is coming this close to being thrown out of the family,' says Majella, holding up her fingers as if to illustrate, to clueless cooks, a pinch of salt.

Lucky Jax, thinks Caryl, who then immediately feels guilty. This in turn triggers an urge to gorge on chocolate. Caryl is sitting in her car, hoping to reverse out of the family compound. Furious Majella, standing on the doorstep with Parkin the red setter close at hand, has yet to finish getting things off her eminent chest. There is insurance to cover the cancellation—the bride's instability of mind will be cited, 'one pheasant short of a brace' to use Majella's exact words—but this is about more than the money. Majella's latest canapé creations—the seeds perhaps of a future book on party planning—will go untasted. But above all, there is the dismantling of the myth of the happy family.

Caryl knows that Majella sets immense store by the notion of the happy family. After all, the family that eats together, stays together. She knows how desperately her mother wants Britain to believe in the construct she has created of well-nourished bliss. Because a mother's love is demonstrated through the food she provides.

But lately, in amongst the ethnic throws and joss sticks of her therapist's consulting room, Caryl has become aware that the *food as love* thing is all an act. The unspoken code of 'I feed you therefore I love you' implicit in breastfeeding has become warped along the way. Majella's need to cook comes from an even greater need to comfort *herself*. She is ravenous for the compliments; I feed you therefore you will love *me*.

'Don't worry about Jax,' says Caryl, not for the first time.

And her mother, not for the first time, fails to take the cue. 'A wedding breakfast doesn't just make itself, you know.'

'I know. And you've put in so much effort.'

'And she hasn't even had the decency to phone.'

And you wonder why, thinks Caryl.

Caryl is still in her car, and Majella is still on the doorstep. The space between the two is wide and empty. It ought to be so simple, thinks Caryl, to go over and hug my mother as I hugged Jax earlier this morning. Caryl loves Jax unreservedly. She loves her messy hair, her dainty hands, her gung-ho spirit, and her obsession with cupcakes. She loves her in a big sisterly, you stole my first proper make-up kit but I'd still die for you way. Two years apart, as children they were staunch allies against Majella's nightly diet of moussaka, brinjal curry, zucchini bake, or pissaladière, with Caryl regularly in awe of Jax voicing the heresy that Majella's meals were vile and smelly and that what they really wanted for supper was Heinz baked beans.

What Caryl feels for Majella is less clear. Majella is unreachable, like a culinary technique known only to chefs with Michelin stars. She's a cook because she prefers to feed herself. As a child, continuity of supply was Majella's constant anxiety, which Caryl understands given that Majella's mother skipped out of the family home and into the arms of a Madrilenian lover when her daughter was barely four. I feed you therefore you will love me, irrespective of what happens.

'It's just that I worry about her.'

Caryl stops trying to picture a Madrilenian lover of her own and a life of paella. 'Who?'

'Jacqueline.' Majella pronounces it in the French fashion, as if she speaks of *un receipt gastronomique* of her own devising which, in a way, of course, Jax is. '*Mon Jacqueline*. Who will look after her now?'

And for a moment, Caryl is shocked that her mother believes Jax needs looking after. Jax who is so sorted, who has done this grown-up thing and defined herself. A woman worthy of more than a cad like Jonty. I am worth this much. Because I'm worth it. Caryl is wary of those sassy little adverts with their empowering straplines because she never feels deserving. The men she meets find her cold and self-sufficient. She doesn't even believe she is worthy of food. The quicker it goes in, the quicker it must come out.

'Are you sure you don't want me to stay? Mum?'

But even as she asks, Majella is bending to speak to Parkin and usher the dog inside, the organic poultry at her chest pendulous and faintly threatening. 'No, darling. Get back to London and have some fun. The marquee will be down in no time and then I've got *Food of Love* matters to review with Parkin here.'

It is Caryl who would like a hug at this moment, now that the meticulously orchestrated order of the day has been disturbed. Now that all the love and romance implied by a wedding have been tossed like vegetable peelings onto the compost heap. But even as she imagines receiving a hug

HUNGRY FOR LOVE

from her mother, she also feels an urge to vomit up her breakfast, ashamed of having ingested food, of having dared to feel hungry, but above all ashamed of her need to want more from the already slender maternal rations available.

IRISH STEW

'…usually mutton. Nowadays lamb is used, and some modern tastes like to add garlic or rosemary for added piquancy. But the essence of the dish is its simplicity and its echo of an era when a meat and vegetable stew was a gift from the gods during times of hardship…'

Jax's hands shake so much she can barely turn the ignition. In her head she hears on a loop Jonty's threats to come round and cause serious bodily harm. It's as though by her decision to take control of her life she has stepped into the world of sink estates where violence is the only solution, whatever the problem. And perhaps not just sink estates. Beyond the elegant railings next to where she is currently parked, she can hear the Trustafarian toddlers in the garden square, playing war games, carving up territory. The noise confirms: we are boys and we fight for what we want. She is standing her ground for a life without Jonty, but she is underpractised in battle.

As her car kicks into life, she hears Jonty's roar into the far end of the square, having broken the land-speed record from his flat. She executes an unfortunate four-point turn and Jonty gives chase. St George's Drive, Lupus Street, the Embankment and a swing left, over Chelsea Bridge, and Jonty's Aston Martin is now roaring down the wrong side of the road. Cars coming the other way flash him, in vain. He's now parallel to Jax, soft top down on this, the perfect day for a wedding, his wedding. He yells comments best kept to the trading floor.

A policeman on a motorbike roars up behind the Aston Martin and flags it down. Jax is now able to pull away. It's only when waiting at the next traffic lights that she has time to think about what to do next. Given that most of her friends have made plans to be somewhere in Sussex, for a certain someone's nuptials, who else is there left in London that Jax knows?

Mike opens the door to his flat, but keeps the chain on. Through the slit Jax spies a sitting room floor littered with the telltale white lids and silver cartons of a take-away. Stray snippets of chow mein noodles stuck to Mike's jumper suggest it was a Chinese.

'Ah,' he manages to say, when he sees that it's Jax. She watches his eyebrows slide closer together. 'Come in.'

He follows her into his lounge. 'I get it. You're trying to be fashionably late for your own wedding.'

Jax shakes her head.

'You want me to give you away?'

'Don't be daft.' She is briefly unnerved that at this riposte Mike looks almost crestfallen. 'I told you on the phone, I've called it off.'

Mike blinks. 'So why are you here?'

At which point Jax bursts into tears. The fact that the answer to this question is 'because I have nowhere else to go', strikes Jax as a seismic thing for one person to say to another. Especially when The Other is so misanthropic. Mike famously regards women crying as the physical embodiment of nails scraping down blackboards. But Jax is weeping for several minutes before she realises that Mike hasn't moved or said *anything*. Nothing at all. She's not begging Mike to lay teddies and flowers at her feet, but a hug would be nice.

And then Jax senses movement. Through the wet blur she can see that Mike has crossed to his sofa, remote control in hand. Immediately the TV is silent. And Jax is left with the thought that, given the nature of the man, this is the most loving, most compassionate gesture that someone like Mike could have made.

'So, you've come to beg for your job back?'

Jax swallows. In the drama of deciding whether to kick her fiancé into touch, Jax has completely forgotten that a month ago she resigned from *Your Day*. Only a life of gym-punctuated indolence, having Jonty's babies and eating moreish morsels from the Barracks Bakery lay ahead.

'Has Kitty–?'

'Yes, Kitty from *Blushing Brides* has accepted. She starts in three weeks time, the day you were due back from honeymoon–.' Mike's face breaks into a smile. It's never good when Mike smiles. He smiles the way Jax played the piano as a child: badly, because the skill was practised so infrequently. Jax reaches for one of his mismatched scatter cushions and clutches it for comfort.

'Well, I think it's obvious what you should do,' Mike says, lighting a cigarette.

'Not to me it isn't.'

'Well, you've already booked time off for your honeymoon, so maybe you should use the time to go abroad, write a piece for *Your Day*, and try and win your job back.'

'But it already is my job. Tell Kitty the slot is no longer vacant.'

'Human Remains,' says Mike, with a shrug, as if, legally, the human resources department of a company wields all the power.

While Mike inhales, Jax contemplates smothering Mike with the cushion. Dumping her fiancé has unleashed homicidal tendencies.

HUNGRY FOR LOVE

'–and it's an area *none* of the other magazines *ever* cover–'

'None of them?' Jax says, to cover up the fact that, in her fury, she hasn't been listening.

'None of them. It would be a first. *Your Day* would be hailed as champions–'

He goes into what Conrad has dubbed Mike's 'orator mode', when he gets very impassioned.

'–as *Your Day* is seen to fight for the rights of–'

'Of–?' Jax repeats, hoping Mike will repeat something too, like the important bit of the previous sentence.

'The broken.'

'What?'

'The broken. Like I said, I want you to do a feature on post-break-up destinations.'

'But we're a wedding magazine. People buy *Your Day* because they're planning a marriage, not planning a break-up.'

'But that's it. It's perfect. Consider it a try-out for your old job.'

Jax's mouth tightens—like a cat's bum—as though to stop even the idea penetrating. No husband and no job. Can the day get any better?

'Conrad's already booked on the trip. In fact he's flying out tonight. You go with him, and we can save money on the room.'

'You want me to share a room with Conrad?'

Jax sees that Mike has stubbed out his cigarette, as if the idea is so seminal, so revolutionary, it requires a lifestyle statement such as giving up smoking. 'It's perfect. Just think how many articles we can get out of this one activity holiday!'

'Remember when I went to Wales to cover that kyaking company which organizes ladette hen weekends? I came back with a dislocated toe.'

IRISH STEW

Mike clears his throat. 'Well, it's not that sort of activity holiday.'

Jax narrows her gaze. 'What kind of activity holiday is it, then, that doesn't cause dislocated toes?'

Mike digs around in the pocket of his jeans for another ciggie. 'I can't remember,' he says, tapping a fag on the box. 'You'll find out when you get there,' he adds, lamely, knowing he is caught.

'Jax takes a step towards him. 'Tell. Me.'

'It's a cookery course,' he mumbles, lighting up.

'A cookery course! You want me to apply for my own job by writing about cooking? You have to be bloody joking?' Although Jax can tell by the short drags that her boss is not. 'But I can't cook.' Jax's voice is an octave higher than usual.

'I know. I've seen the microwave at work after you've tried reheating pizza. The point is: do you want to learn? Do you want to unleash your inner Jamie Oliver?'

'Do *you*?' Jax retorts, kicking at the carton containing the remains of last night's sweet-and-sour pork balls. 'Maybe you're the one who should go with Conrad.'

Mike's pale pink lips stretch into two skinless sausages. Not a pretty sight. 'Of course *I* don't ever want to cook, Jax. But then my mother doesn't cast quite the same culinary shadow over my life.'

'That's pathetic. Mike.' Jax adds his name in the vain hope that it might invest her with strength and superiority.

'Oh yeah? Well, I can't cook because I can't be arsed. But you? You've *chosen* not to learn to cook. So what's all that about, eh?'

'And in any case,' says Jax, ignoring the pointedness of Mike's comment 'it's Saturday. And you said Conrad leaves tonight. You'll never get it all organized in time.' She is just about to flounce out of Mike's flat when she hears Jonty's voice from the landing outside, accompanied by a fist on Mike's front door.

Mike puts a finger to his lips and sidles towards the sound.

'Who is it?' he asks.

'Mike, mate. It's Jonty. I need to speak to Jax.'

Mike swivels his gaze to look at her and his mouth twitches into a smile. 'What makes you think she's here? Mate.' Mike nods at Jax, as if to say: that'll show him.

'Well.' Jonty pauses. 'Her car's outside, half-mounted on the pavement, and there's a traffic warden about to stick a ticket on her windscreen.' Mike glares at Jax while Jonty carries on. 'So, I guess she could be visiting a neighbour of yours, but would you mind checking all the rooms in your, er, studio flat and getting her to speak to me? Mate.'

Jax is beginning to wonder whether asserting yourself is ever worth the inevitable aggression, and glimpses a bleak future with no friends and lots of cats. Maybe this is the moment of temporary resistance, that familiar ritual in the clunkiest of movies, before the door opens and she rushes into Jonty's arms forever. She can almost feel his biceps close around her. Their grip tightens. She cannot breathe. The fantasy of getting over Jonty is sliding out of reach.

She looks at Mike. His eyebrows are asking her again what she wants to do. Working together for three years has not made the two of them telepathic. She mouths something at him, but Mike, like most men, has never learned to lip-read.

Jax glances around the shabbiness of Mike's sitting room, for inspiration. As the setting for a pivotal moment in her life, the romantic in her regrets that it doesn't quite live up to billing. She spies one of the white Chinese takeaway lids and picks it up. Smudges of grease have turned it orange. With a grimace, she writes in the oil with an index finger, and holds it up to Mike. He reads it and his face changes.

'Actually, Jonno,' says Mike, addressing the door, 'I have a message for you—'

'Actually, Mike, I'm not interested. You tell her to get out here, now.'

Mike, and Jax loves him for this, has read her four words and can see it all. All that she hasn't told him, all that she hasn't told anyone. Jax's whole life is in those four words. His voice has become measured and deep. 'When I give you the message, you will leave—'

'Feck off.' And Jonty hurls his whole body at Mike's front door.

'Do that again, and I'm calling the police. Do you want Jax's message or not?'

It is hard to argue with a closed door. Beyond it comes the sound of someone cracking their knuckles in impotence. Jonty agrees.

'Then it's goodbye Jonty.'

'What's the message, arsehole?'

Mike looks at Jax. She nods, and turns away. Mike holds up the Chinese takeaway lid, and reads it as solemnly as a religious text. 'Jax knows about Miranda.'

And Jax has the sense that here in this cramped little bachelor pad, far removed from her own Farrow & Ball cashmere loveliness, surrounded by the ancient talismans of the single male—the stacks of LPs and mugs of cold, half-drunk coffee—that her life has now tilted onto a slightly different axis.

CAPPUCCINO CUPCAKES

'...the most playful of combinations, where the sponge cake can be speckled with vanilla or coffee. Similarly, the buttercream could be a mascarpone cheese version, or espresso-flavoured frosting to complement the cake. Either way, the fun is in the taste-and-flavour contrast between base and topping, which adds a playful...'

Jax enters the Barracks Bakery, to be cleansed of distress. She steps into the deeply familiar wood-and-brick interior and inhales the fug of cloves and cinnamon and yeasty aromas. She quivers with pleasure. Soon her other senses will be cheered by the damp density of sour cream sponge. She could be on a morphine drip, Dan's cakes are so reliably therapeutic. In her preoccupation she doesn't see the other customers in the shop, alerted to her arrival by the jingling of a tiny bell above the door, but heads for the counter.

Sonya is taking money at the till. She is also standing close to Dan. A bit too close, Jax thinks. Presumably it's a love thang, an 'office romance'.

Dan is slicing into a chocolate loaf. Jax detects admirably high levels of concentration. And it occurs to her that Dan has possibly the dream job—a vocation—cutting cakes for a living. It may be an ordinary occupation, but it certainly doesn't have the demeaning qualities of Jonty's rapacious calling.

Dan's practised hand is steady on the knife. It's a hand scattered with light, inviting freckles, like his face and arms and—Jax supposes—the parts of his body she has never seen beyond his rolled up Viyella sleeves, his camouflage-print apron, and his astonishing range of corduroy trousers. It's

CAPPUCCINO CUPCAKES

as though he dusts his body with the scrumptious caramel powder he sprinkles on the cafe coffees and which he grinds himself daily from Caramac bars. Freckles she has a sudden urge to stroke, to join up the dots. Enough! She thinks. Time to starve myself of men. After Jonty's behaviour, they are nothing more to me than spoiled milk.

Dan looks up and has to stifle a gasp. He's astonished to see in his bakery the very woman who for the past year or so has taken up residence in his head. His skin heats up. Like Angus, Dan has worked out the underlying reason for this apparition, if not the specifics. But unlike Angus, Dan oozes tact and discretion.

With a subtle nod to a nearby table, Dan gestures to Jax to sit down while he fulfils the chocolate loaf order. In his head, he's computing possibilities—Dan has been trained to think twenty moves ahead, to clear surrounding areas, to save lives—as to why Jax is, on this of all mornings, not in Sussex but in his bakery. Who says miracles never happen?

Soon, Dan appears at her table, bearing a tray of cakes, khaki napkins at the ready. He watches her stare at the tray, where two cupcakes sit—peanut toffee and cappuccino; his money is on her eating the cappuccino one first—her eyes filling with tears. He then retreats, ostensibly to mend a hinge to a cupboard door beneath the counter, but in truth to observe. The old bomb disposal mantra returns: the absence of the normal and the presence of the abnormal means it's suspicious; if it's suspicious, it stays suspicious until normality returns.

He watches her first dig out her phone from her handbag and read the screen. She must have had a voicemail because she then presses a button, puts to the phone to her ear and listens. And he is still watching as her expression sags. The wedding is obviously off. How dare that bastard hurt her. His heart is racing as he tries to decide whether or not to approach her and ask if she's OK. It's when he sees her reach for the cappuccino cake that he knows he has to act.

A slight scrape of the wooden stool, and Dan sits down alongside her at the moment she takes a bite. He sees the moment the buttercream blooms in her mouth, followed by the crumb of the cake, the two melting into one. Like receiving kisses.

'Thank you,' she finally says, taking a bite.

'Is it all right?' Dan's forehead has creased.

'Of course. Your cakes are divine.'

Dan's smile is cautious. 'Yeah. But something's not quite working with the cappuccino. I don't know what it is.'

Jax hesitates.

'Go on. Tell me.' His back stiffens, but he really values Jax's opinion.

'Well. But no. What do I know?'

'You enjoy eating. That makes you the perfect critic.'

'Ah. Nothing's ever perfect!'

Only you, thinks Dan.

Jax takes another bite, gently nudging the marzipan coffee bean out of the way with her teeth. She grins as she chews, but Dan's stare does not let her go. He genuinely wants her thoughts.

'OK. Don't be offended, but I've often thought: that, you know, that maybe the marzipan decoration is a sweet hit too far.'

'Ditch the marzipan?'

CAPPUCCINO CUPCAKES

'Mmmmm,' she nods, chewing.

'So no decoration?'

She swallows. 'You could use a real coffee bean instead. Its bitterness would go winningly with the buttercream–'

God, I'm beginning to sound like one of my mother's recipes. Not that Majella writes the text herself. She has someone called Mandy write all her flowery prose.

'Bitter. Of course!' Dan reaches into his apron for a notepad and scribbles down Jax's suggestion. He even underlines it. 'Might it then become your favourite?'

'How do you know it isn't already?'

'Ha! It's my job to know. Who buys what. How many. Variations on buying patterns–'

Jax feels quite cheered to hear there might be buying patterns in cakes. And if there are rules about cakes, then maybe there are rules for love. After all, there are some days when only carrot cake will do. 'Do I have a buying pattern?'

Even beneath the freckles a faint blush is visible. 'Oh, it's just a silly bit of pop psychology I've mixed in with my layman's market research. Take no notice.'

Jax recalls buying chocolate velvet cupcakes with extra heart sprinkles after Jonty proposed—which was either coincidence or hormonal. The thought of that weekend in Venice now makes her stomach churn. 'Seriously, tell me what I buy when.'

Dan clears his throat. 'You always order cappuccino when you, you know, when you need comforting.'

He watches as a tear slides down Jax's nose, and passes her a napkin.

'Sorry, it's been horrendous. It's just—it's just I hurt so much.' She blows her nose.

HUNGRY FOR LOVE

Which is how Dan finds out about Miranda and Jonty and the cancellation of today's nuptials by remote.

'That's horrendous. How on earth did you find out they were having an affair?'

In that instant he sees Jax's face cloud over and regrets crossing the line.

'I can't really say. It would get someone into a lot of trouble. And now,' she adds, 'my phone's completely clogged with voicemails. I've had one from my sister Caryl, confirming that she's done the deed and told my mother I've dumped Jonty, and now at least a dozen from my mother threatening to drive up to London and drag me back down the aisle. And not only that, but one guest, on Jonty's side, naturally, is curious to know whether he can get his money back from JustWeddingGifts.com.'

'Bloody cheek.'

'And if so, how quickly.'

'Tell him you've put all the gifts on eBay.'

'Brilliant idea. For charity, of course.'

'Of course. But that you don't hold out much hope of his gift reaching its reserve because it's so inferior to all the others.'

Jax gasps in delight. Just then, her phone beeps and they both look at the screen, Dan from sideways on. Jax's face falls. She presses a few buttons. 'Jonty's texts are curt and unrepeatable. I'm taking an infantile pleasure in deleting them. In fact, the only person whose day I've obviously made is the Battersea traffic warden when I parked outside my boss's flat on the pavement.' She chomps away at more cappuccino cupcake until only the paper casing is left.

'No need to ask if you're eating properly.' Jax sticks her tongue out at him and Dan passes her another paper napkin. 'Although I'm hurt you feel the need to add extra salt to my buttercream. You're ruining my recipe!'

She grins through the tears. It's the sting to her facial muscles that makes her realise that she hasn't laughed properly for months. Fleetingly she wonders what it would be like to be stroked by that freckled hand, to fall asleep in those freckled limbs. Although to cast about for male company not six hours after formally jettisoning one's fiancé, surely screams rebound if not insanity.

'Dan, can I ask you something?'

Shit. He wants to say no. He has actually had dreams where he imagines talking to Jax for the rest of his life, but in truth he hasn't talked to anyone about real feelings for—well, ever. He ought to be getting back to his clients. He should definitely say no. 'Sure. Fire away.'

'Do you think I've done the right thing, dumping Jonty at the altar?'

In his lap Dan crushes the remaining napkins in his fist. Surely she doesn't still want the prick back? He can only think of one thing, one mature thing to say and it's the one thing he really, really doesn't want to ask. 'I guess that depends on whether you still love him?' His heart has started racing again.

Jax looks up at Dan. 'You would tell me, wouldn't you, if you thought I've been selfish?'

'Selfish? How can standing up to the person who betrayed you ever be regarded as selfish behaviour?'

But Jax doesn't answer. Instead she laughs nervously. 'And as if my day, my life, couldn't get any worse, my boss is forcing me to go on a cookery holiday. Tonight. I'm still not sure how to wriggle out of it.'

HUNGRY FOR LOVE

Dan's eyes widen, his lashes becoming a row of strawberry blonde exclamation marks. 'You're being paid to travel and cook? What's not to like?'

'But I can't cook.' Two little spots of embarrassment rouge her cheeks, like apricot icing.

Dan stops with his hand midway through his sandy hair. 'You once told me you couldn't make toast, but I assumed you were exaggerating!'

Jax pulls a face. Please don't say, If you can read, you can cook.

'Not at all?'

Jax shakes her head and juts out her lower lip.

Dan fumes at an innate sense of decency which stops him kissing those perfect raspberry-red lips. Even if they belong to someone who can't cook. He must have misheard her. 'You can boil an egg, surely?'

'I was in a home economics class once and my egg refused to scramble. Instead it dribbled off the plate and onto Miss Smith's open-toed sandals. However, I do know,' she adds, 'the phone numbers of six curry houses off by heart.'

'So wouldn't this be a great opportunity to learn? Collect recipes? For free?'

'You haven't met my colleague Conrad. As loathsome colleagues go, he's the most loathsome.'

'I did read an article once about something called Office Rage, but it made no sense. How bad can colleagues be?'

Jax describes Conrad's more noxious habits: throwing phones, shouting at juniors, being rude. 'He is so self-absorbed he even claimed on expenses a Burberry mac after we'd arrived to cover a wedding fair and found it was raining.'

CAPPUCCINO CUPCAKES

'Does everyone who works in an office get stressed?'

Jax nods.

'So why do people do it?'

'I don't know. For many people, office life is all they know. People are scared to leave their comfort zone. I think that's another reason why I feel so wobbly. Not only have I dumped my boyfriend but inadvertently I've got to fight to get my old job back. Have you ever left a job?' she adds.

Dan thinks back to the day he received the telegram about his father's death. He'd been walking to a cafe with a couple of Afghan Army soldiers, to meet up with Gunner Bill. To say what, he didn't know. Probably to say nothing about his father, but just to have his mate alongside him as he sipped a glass of chai. He remembers the crack and the flash and then the flames and the black smoke. And the silence that seemed to last forever, before the screams. And all that time—clearing the streets of people, helping with the injured, waiting in the blistering sun for the relief vehicles—deep in Dan's pocket had nestled the telegram from his mother. A telegram to her only child. He could picture her drafting the telegram, arranging the chopping of the tree for Dad's coffin, sitting watching the nightly news for an update on Afghanistan, all on her own. And he knew then that he had to leave the army, that he couldn't do this job anymore. If the IEDs or the Taliban didn't get you, accidents might.

He nods slowly, deliberately.

And for several minutes, they sit in companionable silence.

And if I hadn't left the army, thinks Dan, I'd never have met you.

IN—FLIGHT DINING

'…and which play havoc with sleep patterns and digestion. So it's a good idea to take with you foods to snack on during a flight, such as these easy-to-make, easily portable energy bars which contain seeds and…'

'Mike did *what*?' seethes Conrad, after Jax has tracked him down to the business class lounge, a privilege courtesy of the holiday company keen to ensure amazing press coverage.

Across the crowded room, she saw Conrad's bald head gleaming under the halogens. How many times in the office had Jax longed to grab a biro and scribble *Conrad's Head* all over that conceited egg-shaped dome? Beyond the clusters of CEOs and cruise-wear wives, Conrad was pouring himself a martini. With time to kill until boarding, Conrad was relaxed. Not a care in the world. Conrad was not expecting Jax.

'Mike did *what*?' When incensed, Conrad's voice acquires the vibrations of a tuning fork. A businessman, spooning olives on to a saucer, knocks them to the floor.

'But Mike promised me. This was supposed to be *my* trip, *my* bonus, *my* reward–'

'Your reward for what?'

'For putting up with you!' he sneers, gulping at his martini. 'Hang on a minute,' he then says, leering. 'Hold on, just one minute. Your text!'

Jax mentions something about duty-free and turns sharply.

'No you don't.' He grabs Jax's arm and whispers, 'you've wangled yourself this little trip because you've been dumped, haven't you?'

IN-FLIGHT DINING

It occurs to Jax that Conrad must have a sister called Bitchy Bev.

In the cabin, Conrad assumes the aisle seat. He makes a point of sticking his long limbs out in the aisle and refuses to flirt with the middle-aged stewardesses. An ugly childhood has left Conrad with a deep fear that people might think him genuinely desperate.

Jax gazes out the window at the foreshortened ground staff in their fluorescent jackets. They load luggage or stand holding hoses, observed by others clutching clipboards. And she is reminded of Jonty. Making love with Jonty, she realizes, was very much by the book. Although it was hardly lovemaking. It was sex; all gong and no dinner. Jonty on top, once a week, with a quick doggie style for dessert. Given that men apparently think about sex every six seconds, Jax still assumes such lack of originality was her fault, despite the fact that she had once even endured a Brazilian. In fact, Jonty's disinterest in her trimmed topiary had been the first clue that something illicit might be up, as though his gardener's eye was already in, as it were. And it's not as though Jax doesn't possess a vivid sexual imagination. But her suggestion to try the fabulously naughty things Daniel Craig does to her in her dreams had been met with a scoff and a curt instruction to turn over.

The sun sinks low, diffusing its usual glow. These are the lyrics from a song on a loop in the cabin. The vast sky turns gold, then pink, then vermillion. Desmond, an amateur poet, used words like vermillion. It is only in the tight air of the plane that Jax realizes that the person she misses most right now is her dad.

HUNGRY FOR LOVE

He died, in true Desmond style, without fuss. One minute he was eating a meal, lovingly prepared by his famous wife, the next he'd slipped under the table and was struggling to breathe. Jax suspects that after today's events, Desmond would have been quietly—obviously quietly, Desmond was the epitome of mild, the yoghurt to his wife's vindaloo—applauding the emergence of his daughter's inner resolve. Applauding while not a little envious, perhaps.

And nervous—the fact that Jax is now single again would have resurrected in Desmond earlier worries that his little girl would remain lost and unprotected forever.

BREAKFAST SMOOTHIES

'...most important meal of the day. But with so many of us leading busy lives, smoothies are a great way to eat something quick and nutritious for sustained energy throughout the morning. I've updated my old recipe to include soaked chia seeds and linseeds for extra...'

Dan is out for a run. Last night, he didn't sleep a wink. What he wouldn't do to that bastard Jonty should he ever dare cross the threshold of the Barracks Bakery.

And as Dan's battered trainers pound the pavement, he has a glimpse of an old life, of stag-rutting masculinity, of hand-to-hand combat and fierce camaraderie. His military family. A life he had willingly left behind and isn't sure he could recapture, even if he wanted to. Yet he doesn't think he has felt this angry, and yet this helpless, since he witnessed the crackle and the flash and the end of Gunner Bill.

God, what should he have said, when Jax had sprung that question on him? It's been going round and round in his head all night long. Did he sound supportive enough, sufficiently understanding? Or in his desire not to let his true feelings show, had he sounded—God forbid—disinterested? What he is sure of, after twelve hours of one-sided debate on the matter, is that he was right not to blurt out, I'm as jealous as hell and am punching the air that you've kicked that dickhead Jonty into touch. No, that would have been way too much, way too soon.

And yet he still can't believe how personal their conversation had turned, how open she had been. Maybe this means Jax trusts him. Or maybe it just means she sees him as a rock, a safe shoulder to cry on. Until the next Jonty comes along. Shit.

Through the clean windows of the desirable residences he glimpses the faces of couples and families at breakfast, and is gripped by an almost unbearable loneliness. His feet pound on.

CALIFORNIAN SUSHI ROLL

'...with the trend for Japanese cuisine. This easy-to-make roll is created inside out, with the seaweed casing now inside with the filling, and with an outer casing of seeds such as sesame. Now such rolls feature on menus across the globe, and not just on America's West Coast.'

Jax is taking a little exercise. The hotel boasts multiple jogging tracks through the surrounding pine trees and Jax is deriving a certain steady comfort from knowing that whichever route she takes, she will eventually end up back at the hotel lobby with its piped muzac, its glacial air conditioning and its life-size straw donkey-with-sombrero.

It is now twenty-six hours since Jax sent her explosive texts. Twenty-six hours since she set in motion events which have sent her life down a different path, not to say appalled Majella and abruptly altered the weekend plans of two hundred people. It is ten minutes since she discovered that the elusive sheep in this rocky part of the world sensibly wear bells around their neck so that lost ones can be found and brought home safely, bells that jingle at a mellow pitch which is soothing rather than annoying. And it is twelve hours since she was forced to confront the reality of sharing a bedroom with Conrad.

Jax has quickly evolved an easy rhythm of pace which settles the mind and allows her thoughts to float free. As she jogs, she starts to wonder who she is, this newly single person of decisive mind. Like the unfamiliar twig-strewn path beneath, there is something precarious about this new state of being. She knows how to breathe, in the sense that her body is still otherwise functioning normally, but not how to love. You can't nowadays even be engaged and expect your fiancé to behave in a loving manner. And now that she is sworn off men, starving herself of their duplicity and casual cruelty, there exists presumably an inner Jax, previously filled with romantic notions and marital ambition, which will require feeding. Now where's that damned recipe?

Still, it could just be the feel-good endorphins from the morning jog but, in the bell-augmented air, Jax thinks she might even be feeling happy. It has only been twenty-six hours, but already Jonty is receding. Jonty, with his flash car and his bit on the side. She knows it will take time. For example, she catches herself from time to time dreading, with a lurch in her stomach, a wedding that will now never take place. There's always a time lag with thoughts and behaviour. A year ago, a postbox was removed from the street beyond her window at work. Even now, people turn up to post a letter and she watches as they perform a tight pirouette to find it: I know it was here somewhere. Somehow the end, the loss of something they thought fixed, has shaken their world.

The prospect of losing the life she had with Jonty has been similarly destabilising. When she had first worked out Jonty's relationship with Miranda, it was as though a meat skewer had been plunged into her diaphragm. It was a wound which haemorrhaged energy and confidence with every movement she made. The undemanding future she had imagined—of cuddling on the sofa, teaching their children to walk, holding hands in their old people's home—had crashed instantly, and she had spent several days in shock, wearing the same clothes to work for a week.

CALIFORNIAN SUSHI ROLL

Letting go of Jonty has also meant letting go of foodie fantasies. Jonty makes so much money that his investments include London restaurants. At first, Jax didn't notice that every time they went out for supper, they always got the best tables and ate off-menu. After years of her mother's aversion to fast food, being given permission to choose her own food every night quickly became addictive. Because neither she nor Jonty can cook.

Which is not to say she and Jonty haven't tried. At his flat, Jonty installed a blistering designer kitchen. Acres of walnut cupboards and chrome surrounds, a brushed steel prepping island, a seven hob range cooker with additional wok support, an espresso bar, three sinks, and a fridge-freezer with a television in the door, which could house a family of nineteen. Majella nearly fainted when she saw it, when she popped up to London last October to sign books at Hatchards. If she could have moved in that night she would have—not into the flat, into the kitchen.

So, without really being aware of it, Jax fell not just for Jonty but also for a life where she had permission to eat her favourite food. With Jonty, it was as if she was being told you can have whatever you want because you're worth it.

Because now she knows that this is exactly how Jonty lives his life.

And yet here she is, striding along in the morning warmth, grinding loose pine needles into submission, feeling a hint of exhilaration. Jax thinks of her father: steady, kind. The sort of man who used to set aside worms for robins when digging the garden. Desmond, she is sure now, would not have taken to Jonty. Too selfish, too unkind. Maybe it's a generational thing, but Desmond would have wanted a husband for Jax who above all else was kind. There is not, Desmond would often worry aloud, enough kindness in the world.

'Are you alright?'

She has turned a corner and almost tripped over a man leaning awkwardly against a tree. His limbs, especially against the whitest of sports clothes, are impossibly tanned, but his face is closer to puce. His eyelids are half-closed in what Jax recalls could be sexual ecstasy, but clearly here is not. And he certainly isn't taking a breather in order to admire the view.

'I said, do you need help? Are you OK?'

His breath comes in shallow pants. He also has yet to make eye contact as though, like a child, by ignoring her, he might pretend she isn't present to witness his humiliation. Standing still, her jogger's heart still pumping, Jax is aware of the scent of crushed pine needles competing with this man's sweat.

'Do you want to sit down? Might make you feel better.'

The man slumps to the base of the tree, but still doesn't, cannot, look at her. She thinks he looks less flushed and hopes this is a good thing. But she can't leave him like this—for one thing, he lacks a soothing bell around his neck for attracting attention—and so she stays on the path and studies him. He is in his mid-forties, she reckons, with a good head of hair, thick and straight and dark, although greying at the temples. He is kitted out in coordinated branded gym-wear, which hints at an expensive bachelor lifestyle. He probably works in insurance. As well as the cookery school, there is an international insurance conference going on at the hotel, with lapel badges on trestle tables and welcome cocktails tonight in the Salon Don Quixote.

CALIFORNIAN SUSHI ROLL

At one point the man creases over and rests his hands on his knees. Jax notices that the fingers squeezing the joints are ringless, although this signifies very little: Jonty was refusing to wear jewellery after the wedding. Posh Peter had thought he was mad, and claimed that women fancy men in wedding rings precisely because of the implied challenge of forbidden fruit. Either that, or because a ring implies that another woman has already conducted a thorough vetting process, which saves time. Jax, whose heart has now calmed down to the rhythm appropriate for someone not moving, feels it lift a little at the thought that Posh Peter need never be in her life ever again.

'Thank you,' wheezes the man. 'But you, like, don't have to stay.'

Jax detects an American accent. 'Well, I can't really leave you. What if something happened?'

'Something *has* happened.' He says this with an attempt at a laugh. The man has very straight teeth, which surely confirms his transatlantic provenance.

'Well, I'm not leaving you on your own, so if you don't want to move just yet, that's fine, but I'm staying here.'

'Jesus, are you always this determined?'

No, thinks Jax. It's just something in my stars, these past twenty-six hours.

She introduces herself. The lapsed jogger is called Brian, and he lives in California.

Brian clutches his chest, winces and closes his eyes.

'Does it still hurt?'

'Just keep talking to me. Distract me.'

'So do you run much at home?'

Brian finds the energy to raise an eyebrow at the implied suspicion of ill health. 'I'm a member of gyms on four

61

continents. Their aerobic class schedules are all in here,' he adds, tapping his skull. 'Although I'm more of a Pilates man, actually.'

Jax tries to suppress the image of Brian in revealing lycra and leggings, dreaming of having the lead role in an Eric Prydz pop video.

With effort, Brian stands up, so that Jax sees he has urgent eyes with fierce blue irises. 'And I always carry a travel Swiss ball for hotels, like this one, with inadequate gyms.'

Inadequate gyms! Jax doesn't tell him that this is the first hotel she has stayed in with not only a gym but also iPod docks in all the rooms and a pillow menu. Presumably Jonty saved those particular temples of amenity overkill for weekends with Miranda.

'Ah, but do more adequate hotels have their own flock of sheep with bells on?'

'They're not sheep, Jax, they're goats.'

Jax glances down the hill despite knowing, from previous attempts to locate the source of the tinkling, that these animals are too well camouflaged. 'How can you tell the difference?'

'Ah, that's the point. In this stony part of the world, they all look the same, skinny little hairless things. Which is why the ancient Biblical parable of the sheep and the goats works so well.'

'It does? Who says it doesn't?'

'I'm just saying, there's a lot of theological interpretation about why the sheep go to heaven and the goats to hell.'

Brian is the last person she would have imagined knowing this kind of information. If she were with Jonty now, he would smile condescendingly at Brian, and jog on.

CALIFORNIAN SUSHI ROLL

'We had the parable at school, but I've forgotten it.'

'The point of the story is that God is dividing up a mixed group of creatures who outwardly look the same. He's saying that, externally, you can't tell who are the good guys and who are the bad.'

Just like Jonty, then. Outwardly flawless, inwardly rotten. A wave of coldness washes over her. Perhaps Brian is not in insurance after all, but the church. Jax isn't quite sure she is ready for an ecclesiastical discussion but as a refuge from the bad things of this world, faith is known to have previous form.

Like Jonty has form: cheat on me once, more fool you; cheat on me twice, more fool me. 'Reminds me of my mother's test for bad eggs. Fresh eggs sink to the bottom and lie compliantly on their sides. Bad eggs have too much air in them which makes them float if placed in a jug of water.' Jonty, Jax reckons, is most definitely a floater.

She and Brian are now walking slowly along the path. In places it is not quite wide enough for two and their respective biceps have become repeatedly acquainted. A certain dizziness overcame him back there which he puts down to jetlag. Brian loves travel and loves Urup the best. He settles in to telling her about himself and luckily for him, his chance audience is good at listening. She interviews people for a living, although her genuine interest in them and their stories is often irrelevant. At *Your Day*, Mike likes edginess and drama and conflict, but it is hard to weave much of this into a chat, say, with a man who makes sugared almonds. Mike, she feels, should really be somewhere like *Commando* or *Fast Cars* or, at a pinch, *Rugby Monthly*.

HUNGRY FOR LOVE

'I dumped my fiancé yesterday,' she announces to Brian, right in the middle of his detailed description of the worst spas to stay at in Thailand.

'Jesus. I was right the first time. You *are* some kind of ball-breaker.'

Strangers, thinks Jax, can do this. Define you after barely meeting. 'Possibly. I have recently discovered untapped reserves.'

'Whoa—I've met girls like you in Rio. They slip something in your drink, bonk you senseless and run off with all your money. Poor guy.'

'Hey, you've never even met Jonty–'

'Jonty?! Oh my Lord! It's like something out of P.G. Wodehouse. How on earth could you dump someone so quintessentially English?'

'He was part-Irish actually, but thanks for your support,' she laughs. 'And if you must know, he cheated on me.'

'Ah. Never a good move.' And Brian's mouth turns up at one side, as if recalling relevant information. 'So now you're happily single?'

Jax thinks for a moment. 'I'm working on the happy bit.'

'Listen, don't be sad. Think of this time as your Happiness Opportunity.'

The West Coast self-help sincerity of Brian's comment makes Jax grin.

'So, what are you going to do now? I mean, is that why you're here, to work out what to do next?'

'Sort of. I feel like one of those Soviet citizens who grew up praising Stalin all the time and now has a whopping great hole where an ideology should be.'

CALIFORNIAN SUSHI ROLL

'Well, at least that gives me an excuse not to marry you instead. They don't allow commies into the States. Even metaphorical ones.'

So maybe not a vicar, then. Or at least not one forced to be celibate. Or only if his religion involves jetting round the world to save the fallen women of Rio and Bangkok.

By now the hotel's low buildings are in view, sun-blushed and inviting. The Mediterranean air has cooled a little, and a cluster of golfers has gathered outside the entrance to the fitness centre, mincing around on their studded soles. Jax and Brian have arrived at that awkward checkpoint moment of saying goodbye to a stranger.

'Well, thank you for saving my life, English rose.'

His voice reminds Jax of plump fruit. 'Will you be OK now?'

'No, but I'll survive, knowing my guardian angel is somewhere in the building.'

'When my mother was little she prayed for an angel to save her when her own mother left home.' And remembering this story Jax is suddenly filled with tenderness and warmth towards Majella, the child who was abandoned. 'Anyway, I must take a shower.'

'Ok then. See you around. Maybe we should get ourselves some bells.'

'What?'

'Some bells. So we can be found.'

MASHED POTATO

'...ideal comfort food, making it the perfect dish to make when you're planning an early night. The smooth texture is hard to achieve, but the combination of potato, butter and cream are...'

In the corridor Jax passes a room service trolley cluttered with debris, giving off the sleazy smell of ketchup. There's a rose in a vase, manky chicken bones and miniature marmalade pots, which together with smeared plates create a faintly nauseating impression, not of culinary confusion, but of all-day sexual activity. She hurries on past.

Conrad emerges from the bathroom, a towel around his waist, as Jax opens the door. Conrad's chest is damp and muscled. A scent of shower products swirls around him, although a cloud of steam follows him as though he's a pantomime villain. She feels an urge to hiss.

'Did you not think to knock?'

'Conrad, it's my room, too,' she says, waving her credit card-shaped key.

'Well, you stink of sweat.'

Jax contemplates clouting him over the domed head with the bottle of overpriced wine on top of the mini-bar.

Conrad switches on the TV and perches on the edge of one of the twin beds. 'So, what have you been up to? Crying in the woods over your lost love?'

'May I remind you, yet again, that I dumped Jonty, not the other way round?'

'So you say, Jax. So you say.'

66

MASHED POTATO

Later that day, after a quick pasta in the hotel's over-lit coffee shop and a brief, if predictable, scrap with Conrad over territorial rights for the one basin in the bathroom, Jax lies in her bed, her jogger's limbs soothed by the cool sheets.

She hasn't spoken to Majella at all since sending the cancellation text. Throughout the weekend her mother has served up reheated expressions of disappointment and left them on her younger daughter's mobile. She has also not replied to Jonty who in his latest message is threatening to bill her for half the honeymoon. For which he was about to depart, with Miranda, when he made the call. A man whose scruples, clearly, are in inverse proportion to his cash flow. She has, however, sent a text back to Posh Peter who had, as predicted, expressed relief at now being able to watch the Wimbledon women's final—phew!—telling him to *Get A Life*.

She thinks about the local sheep—or are they goats?—with their adorable bells and supreme faith in being found. Caryl often speaks of having been 'found' by her therapist, in the sense that she feels understood by the Jungian One and her clouds of incense and low-wattage lighting. The inference, as Caryl tells it, is that someone earlier should have provided this exquisite form of understanding, the way that mothers can tell the needs of their babies. Being held, says Caryl, with some feeling, occurs on more than just a physical level. As she lies in bed, Jax absently strokes the sun-warmed hairs on her forearms.

Majella has a secure sense of self, or rather she has an identity. She crops up on the kind of quiz shows that take satirical potshots at people in the public eye without much good reason to be there other than her fame from TV cookery shows. And she lives up to the image, the identity of the all-consuming cook, by being pretty hopeless on all the topical stuff, and then coming up with a witty riposte—prescripted, of course—to something which combines an in-depth knowledge of food with an aura of maternal kindness, and which nicely calms the atmosphere after the bitter personal repartee between the team captains.

'Not much call for sous-chefs round here,' is one of her regular lines, delivered drily from under raised eyebrows. There is, the comment implies, only one star on this show. It has become a sort of national catchphrase, especially in the House of Commons.

Originally, out there amongst the pine needles with the insurance world's answer to Eric Prydz, Jax had wondered if it wouldn't be better to jettison trying to find a recipe for love and instead be a sheep—or a goat, obviously—happily cropping meagre supplies of grass before being found. Before yesterday, Jax recognizes she was living a life which pottered along and built up to marrying Jonty, much as mixing milk and eggs with flour leads to pancakes. Today she stands on the threshold of making something else. Add the ingredients in different proportions and you end up not with pancakes but with pastry or a Victoria sponge. And so before she falls deeply into sleep, Jax wonders whether she will ever find the right recipe, and savour the person she is really meant to be.

MISE EN PLACE

'...setting out the ingredients and various utensils to be used in making the dishes, which is the essence of being prepared. This includes chopping vegetables, harvesting herbs, making stocks and sauces and prepping pastry for desserts...'

The cookery school is held in a separate rural building. To reach it, guests must meander down cactus-lined paths through groves of olive trees a thousand years old. The estate is as pretty as its brochures and website imply, and Jax appreciates the absence of trickery. She is trying to take everything in, the flora and fauna, to add colour to the wonderful articles she will write to win her old job back. However, she and Conrad are running late: Conrad took an age in the coffee shop choosing how to have his breakfast eggs ('but are they pan-fried in *safflower* oil?') and the class has already started.

Conrad pushes at a heavy door. Sunlight greets them, dancing on the room's stainless steel surfaces. One wall is of glass and looks on to a view down to the sea which glitters distractingly in the distance. There are three tiers of hip-height benches, with stovetops, sinks and ovens built in. At the front of the class stands a larger bench reversed for teaching. An enormous mirror hangs above it, tilted at an angle, so that the class can monitor what takes place in the saucepans. The class, dressed in a colourful range of European leisure wear, is gathered in front of this teaching stage.

'Ah. You must be Conrad and Jacqueline,' says a smiling man in chef whites at the front of the class. 'You are late because the food, she scares you, no?' And he holds up a knife in the manner of someone ready to chop off the tails of blind mice.

69

HUNGRY FOR LOVE

The rest of the class looks around at the late arrivals and titters.

'But come, come. Bring your good selves. Bring them to me.'

Closer to the bench, Jax can see the chef's name—Pablo—embroidered on his tunic. The batch of would-be cooks stands solemn and attentive, and Jax wonders if she and Conrad haven't by mistake wandered into some kind of cult, with Pablo as the god of the kitchen. She has a glimpse of what it must be like for Majella, in front of the camera, with a rapt audience in the palm of your hand. And she has a flash of childhood memory, of Majella trying to show her how to make gravy and her own gaze roaming disloyally to the climbing frame outside.

'Have you come to save me here, too?' a voice whispers in her ear.

Jax is reminded of melons dripping juice. She spins round to find Brian standing alongside her. 'Do you need saving?'

Brian tips his head in the direction of the kitchen god and winces. 'You should see the size of Pablo's cleaver,' he says.

Brian is—unlike everyone else, in their chinos and polo shirts—wearing a similar tunic to Pablo's, customised with Brian looped in thread around where his left nipple might reasonably be expected to be. Unconsciously she takes a step away. 'I didn't expect to see you here. I thought you were in insurance. Because of the conference. Or even a vicar.'

'Heavens, no!' Brian begins, but Pablo is already calling the class to order.

'So, class. Gather round.' His voice, Jax thinks, possesses the inviting warmth of melted chocolate. 'The world of cooking is about to be unveiled to you in all its glory. This will be a course to relish, a course to consume, a course in which to be seduced

MISE EN PLACE

by food. And by the end, I will have made cooks of you all.'
And he flourishes his knife around in the air, its blade winking
in the sunlight, and Jax surprises herself by imagining that
with one gentle thrust of it he might slice through her clothes.

In the end, it all comes down to the hands. Jax is transfixed
by Pablo's hands, which handle the food on the counter as
one might caress a new lover. First he distributes velvety
peaches and invites the class to stroke the fuzzy skins. Then
he gives out bundles of asparagus and asks them to close their
eyes and brush the tips, to feel the intricate nodules leading
down to the shaft. He does the same for the satiny shells in
a bowl of eggs, and also with a heap of lemons, their grainy
stalks attached. He invites them to score the yielding rinds
with a thumbnail, releasing minute beads of oil, and then
again, with their eyes closed, they are invited to inhale the
fresh citrus scent. Jax sneaks a lick from her fingers and is
rewarded with a tangy sweetness she can't quite define but for
which she knows she has already acquired a weakness.

'Of course, the colours are all wrong,' hisses Conrad
alongside her, his hands fluttering over a small composition
he has created on the bench.

'Conrad, you should get out more. It's a cookery class,
not a still life.'

Jax senses Conrad straightening himself up to his full six
foot two. 'I am a photographer, an artiste. Not some galley
slave.' And he nods in the direction of Pablo, who at that
moment is thrusting a bunch of herbs under his own nose
and staggering around as though intoxicated. The class laughs
at the clowning. Jax looks back at Conrad again, to find him
giving Pablo a look which suggests rolling pins at dawn.

71

HUNGRY FOR LOVE

Gradually Pablo invites them—his style of instruction is smooth and confiding—to break eggs, to whisk them, and to sizzle some butter, chop asparagus, and tip it all into a hot pan. The procedure requires fine timing and a watchful eye: the food could singe at any minute. Everything must be just so, the sharpness of the knives, the size of the pan. And then there's the heat: the butter must melt so that the milk solids and butterfat separate, to turn just this side of nut brown. Too long, a matter of seconds, and it will start to smoke and be too bitter to be of any use other than for meaty fish and alongside chunky flavours like capers.

But as the morning progresses, Jax's embryonic culinary talents do not burst forth. Her work surface becomes encrusted with dried spilt yolk, browning peach slices and smears of butter. As a result, her confidence scrambles and dreams of an award-winning article and a renewed job contract start to evaporate.

She can see nothing of Majella's competence in her hapless fumblings. She slices asparagus pointlessly, the elegant tips never destined to be cloaked in the appropriate luscious emulsions. One particular egg slips out of her hands and she watches horrified as it smashes to the floor, splashing up Conrad's trousers. For a moment she freezes, until she remembers that this is Conrad. Pathetic as she feels this to be, she takes some small pleasure in not confessing.

After a while, Jax stops pretending to cook and instead watches Pablo as he lays shallow bowls out on his workbench. These he fills with liquids of various greens and golds, which shimmer as they catch the light. He stoops to inhale their fragrance. Pablo, Jax observes, has a strong nose, cheekbones weathered like small, ruddy apples, clear eyes shaped by dark brows and a full mouth. Extravagant features, which suggest to Jax that all his senses are alert and finely tuned. The bowls he fills are plain white, brimming with humble oils from the estate. She watches him wiping clean the edges of the bowls as briskly, yet carefully, as if royalty were due. His devotion to the task reminds her of her father.

'Oh goody. Now we can play Guess the Oil,' sighs Conrad, as Pablo invites the class to gather round to taste.

'Does being a killjoy come easily to you, or do you find you have to practice?'

'Ooh, is Pablo our new hero then?' When he is delivering especially spiteful lines, Conrad has a tendency to come over all camp. 'I'll have to warn him you're on the rebound.'

Jax tries to tut and roll her eyes, but an unfortunate image of Pablo feeding her fruit dipped in chocolate has popped into her head and she finds herself hurrying to the teaching bench to mask her flushed face.

A long lunch takes place on a terrace overlooking the sea. A canopy of vines droops with emerald cones of fat grapes. A breeze refreshes after the heat of the kitchen, and in the background Jax imagines she can detect the faint tuning up of the ovine orchestra. Brian pulls up a wrought-iron chair beside her, his plate piled high with wind-dried hams, chargrilled vegetables and wedges of melon kissed with dew. Conrad takes the opposite chair. For someone who hates her so much, Conrad can be annoyingly clingy. Or maybe he's just sadistic.

'Did you know, the pigs for this ham are fed solely on acorns,' says Brian, chewing happily.

'That's all we need. An amateur cook who thinks he's Gordon Ramsay.'

HUNGRY FOR LOVE

'Brian. Have you met my colleague, Conrad?'

Reluctantly, across her plate, the two men shake hands without eye contact—Middle Eastern leaders before a president of the United States—before Brian returns to digging away at his lunch. Conrad picks at his, as if to swallow a morsel from Pablo's kitchen would amount to a betrayal. He informs Brian that Jax cannot cook. Brian replies mildly with a kind smile that this is presumably why she's now on the same cookery course as Conrad. Jax drinks more wine than she had planned to and has to restrain herself from flicking a finger at Conrad's bald crown as she goes up for seconds.

During the afternoon session, the class, faintly sozzled with alcohol, is more subdued. Pablo is able to whizz through several cooking techniques without the usual sprinkling of double entendres and giggling from the cheap seats. His whites are still immaculate and his enthusiasm for food unstinting, his fingers cavorting over various ingredients as they are sliced or whipped or sautéed.

Back at her own cooking station, as Pablo calls it, Jax finds that she is still struggling with the basics such as separating eggs, although the amount of rosé consumed over lunch may be a contributory factor. However, it both annoys and surprises Jax. When she had agreed to Mike's last minute suggestion of the trip, she'd had no idea she would actually want to acquire any of the skills on offer. Pablo, circulating the room, detects her angst and comes to stand behind her. She feels the warmth of his body as it shadows hers.

'How can I help?' he murmurs, in chocolaty tones.

'I don't know. I don't even know what it is I don't know.'

'So, let me see. What do you do for work?'

She tells him about *Your Day*, and having to write articles.

MISE EN PLACE

'So you start each day with a blank sheet of paper?'

'A blank computer screen, but yes.'

Pablo gives one of his expressive shrugs. 'But then this is just like cooking, the fear of the blank page, the blank chopping board, the empty pan. So tell me, how do you write something from scratch?'

'I think of what I want to write, the argument of the whole thing, and then I break it down into smaller units, maybe each paragraph, or each sentence. And then I build it up from there.'

Pablo squeezes her shoulders. 'But this is exactly like my style of cooking. Imagine the final dish, play around with it in your mind and, with the basic tools you learn here, build up your dish from scratch.'

'No recipes?' asks Jax, faintly appalled, thinking of *Food of Love* and her hope to find a recipe for love.

'No recipes. What I will show you is how to cook by instinct, your senses. Learn to feel your way into the food.'

He encircles her arms with his own. The vigour of them quite shocks her. Together they crack an egg shell on the side of the bowl with more force than Jax had assumed was permissible. Then gently, letting the white of the egg drop lugubriously into the bowl, they gracefully transfer the globe of yolk from one half shell to the other until all the white has fallen into a separate bowl, cupping the golden sac as tenderly as if it had actually developed into a baby chick. After a dozen eggs their hands squelch suggestively with albumenal goo. And it occurs to her that if Pablo was one of Dan's cupcakes, he would be the variety Dan devised recently for Valentine's Day, a salacious combination of dark sponge with a molten centre of liquid chocolate and

HUNGRY FOR LOVE

Eat Me scrawled onto the cassis-spiked buttercream. Jax had hoped for one from Jonty but in the end had had to buy herself half a dozen.

With Pablo's hands-on help, Jax's senses become acute. She smells the ripe flesh of the peach, the nasal nuttiness of the melted butter, the whisper of wild garlic, and something fresher, like rain on vegetables. She lets the smells wash over her, as though an understanding of the ingredients is being absorbed through her skin. When Pablo takes his leave from her station, his hand lingers on hers a fraction.

The day's class is drawn to a triumphant close with a mesmerising performance by Pablo involving five saucepans, spun sugar threads and copious slugs of alcohol. Conrad, to be fair, has been taking photographs of everything, so it's just possible that Pablo has been playing up to his two cameras: one for colour and one for Conrad's award-winning black and whites.

She watches Conrad at work. Photography for Conrad is a way of putting the world into little boxes. The image then becomes Conrad's possession, an idea reinforced by the convention that, rather like his yogurts in the office fridge, each photo printed in the magazine must carry his name, his photographer's credit. When Conrad speaks of Jonty dumping Jax, it is yet another manipulation of reality, which sends her into little tizzies of annoyance, and yet perhaps it is only a kink, a clever refraction of light around the truth. It is something she has been mulling for days: by refusing to learn to cook, to stretch herself, maybe she was keeping the relationship with Jonty on pause. By sleeping with Miranda, maybe Jonty was telling her their relationship had gone stale, even before she had sent her definitive text.

STUFFED CHILIES

'...although remember when preparing fresh chilies to wash your hands immediately afterwards. You don't want to rub your eye accidently with fingers that have been chopping or deseeding chilies, otherwise you'll have a nasty surprise!'

Dan is busy taking churros and empanadas out of the oven. Proximity to the Argentinian Embassy prompted him some months ago to research the foods they miss from home. Now its staff flirt with Dan in that effortless way many male and female Argentinians have, while Sonya quietly seethes on the other side of the till.

'I'm meeting up this evening with that chap I met on Match.com,' says Sonya once the morning rush has passed. She isn't actually meeting anyone tonight but she often throws in such titbits to see if she can arouse Dan's interest.

'I thought you'd let your account there lapse after that awful time with the stand-up comedian? The one you reckoned was just mining your life for material?'

Damn, thinks Sonya. I didn't know you were listening when I made that one up.

Dan glances at the clock. With one practised hand he sets a small jug of milk to froth and allows a little coffee to drip thickly into a small cup. A shots-worth is ready just as the postman pushes at the door. Dan lines cup and jug up on the counter as the postman hands him a bundle of letters. Down in one, the postie knocks back the espresso with a dash of milk and then he's back on his round. He shouts out his goodbyes but for once Dan doesn't reply.

HUNGRY FOR LOVE

Dan's hand is shaking. Breezily slicing a paper knife through the envelopes of the bakery's post, he was not expecting to receive a letter like this.

CANAPÉS

'…mustn't be too substantial, not difficult to hold, but small and tasty enough to whet the appetite for the meal to come. Many are salty, to offset the sweetness of wine and cocktails.'

At drinks on the terrace after the class, Jax nibbles on cheese straws spiked with chili and thinks about food, or rather about her aversion to cooking it. She is beginning to believe she needs to understand and accept this about herself if she is to dump it in the dustbin and move on. Not least because for the first time ever, she appears to have arrived at a wonderful, exciting, seductive place where food is about pleasure not power. She came on this course to get Mike off her back and to buy some time, and instead has discovered a wondrous sense of wanting to linger.

It has also been a minor joy to be simply meeting new people. As well as Brian there are those foodies who have attended cookery courses all over the world. They speak of Pablo in reverential terms and have alluded to waiting lists and bribery in order to secure a place here at all. Perhaps Mike pulled more strings to get her here than he has let on. Others envisage improved career opportunities, like the two English girls on the course. They dress in cropped trousers and ballet pumps, and hope to move out of the seasonal world of chalets and into the year-round one of yachts, although Jax suspects their plans would be happily shelved were the right sailor to come along.

There is a barbecue tonight. Jax's mouth is already watering at the smell of charred meat. At her wedding reception, she might have similarly stood clutching a glass of something chilled, holding an architectural canapé, pretending to laugh at Posh Peter's best man speech and feeling a mild unease at her future. Tonight she is amongst strangers and she smiles to feel the tingly glow inside of being part of a new gang.

Brian appears. He is clearly a happy carnivore, his plate piled high with the bones of small animals. Jax selects from a hand-thrown platter another appetizer, a Pablo specialty: aubergine cigars stuffed with whole peeled garlic cloves which have turned meltingly mushy in the oven. She can't quite believe her taste buds, in that she has eaten vegetables and she has eaten garlic before, but never with flavours quite so intense, so realistic as this. Her fingers are almost sore from licking every last drop of juice. It's as though food before was an imitation and now she is experiencing its fabulously true flavours for the very first time.

'How does he do it?' murmurs Jax, dipping a shredded hunk of meat stolen from Brian's plate into a local dish, an orange-zested variant of hollandaise.

'Must have magic fingers,' says Brian, gnawing on a marinated rib. 'Oh look, he's coming this way.' Brian's chin is blood spotted and Jax has a sudden urge to dab it with a napkin.

'I wanted to thank you both for attending my class to-day,' says Pablo, as if their presence had created for him a precious culinary alchemy. He is still dressed in his whites, the fabric remarkably stain free, and is handing round platters of lamb, raspberry pink in the middle. When he stops to talk, Jax and Brian feel almost blessed.

'This food is amazing, Pablo.'

Pablo shakes his head a little—although not so much as to dislodge the praise which Brian has sprinkled on him—

CANAPÉS

and talks about trusting one's instincts over food. At no stage does he say that 'if you can read you can cook', and Jax finds herself wondering what the guru chef, the wunderkind with the whisk, might be like in bed. The word 'basting' pops in to her head for no apparent reason, and she glances in a slight panic at Brian and Pablo to check that she hasn't actually said this out loud. Right now Jax cannot stop linking food to sex. She can barely admit to herself that a few days after dumping her fiancé her unruly subconscious appears to be scouting around for his replacement. It must be the food.

Although food, she knows, can sometimes be a source of distress. For example, she is painfully aware that her sister is not well. Caryl displays the sunken cheeks and dull eyes of a serial regurgitator, which she masks with an over-healthy appetite for calorie-laden foods. Jax has googled eating disorders and understands that there is very little she can do personally. But this doesn't stop her aching inside whenever she sees Caryl looking so shockingly thin. Caryl is trying to write a novel, has even shown Jax a few early chapters. But they are clearly less about telling a racy made-up story, about spies or tank battles or boy-meets-girl, and more about attempts to come to terms with her life as Majella's daughter. The prose is excoriating and the thinly-veiled protagonist cuts herself in intimate places. Jax has privately dubbed it *Look Back in Hunger*. For now, she has suggested Caryl show it not to a literary agent but maybe to her therapist?

Jax comes to from her thoughts about her family to find Pablo staring at her. With a free, if oily, hand he takes one of hers, similarly glistening, and strokes the back of it with his thumb. 'You have the perfect fingers for making pastry.'

Brian almost chokes on his lamb chop.

81

HUNGRY FOR LOVE

Jax perceives the flattery, the chat-up line, for what it is, and yet feels almost dizzy at the soft touch of him skimming her skin. 'Don't be daft. Ready-made was invented for people like me.' There is something more intense about Pablo's voice tonight that makes Jax think of the sweetness of padron peppers with a subtle rasp in the throat at the end of each bite.

'No,' says Pablo, placing the carbonated platter on a nearby surface. 'You are mistaken. Your fingers are so delicate, so long and cool. Pastry needs this feminine touch.' And he gazes at her cuticles so intently she thinks he might be about to lick them.

'So, what's for dessert, Pablo?' asks Brian.

Pablo urges them both to follow him and, leading Jax by the hand, takes them through the crowd of other guests to a table groaning with bowls of fruit and whipped cream. From a small bottle he pours out two glasses of honey-coloured wine and hands them one each. The liquid is sticky on their lips.

'You see, it's the colour of our sunsets here. It's made locally. We call it Rocio Vespertino. Come, let's go and raise a toast to the sun as she sinks below the sea.'

'I'll wait here I think,' says Brian, seizing a slice of nectarine. 'You two go on ahead. I'll catch you up.'

Brian's obvious attempt at discretion gives Jax a moment's hesitation but Pablo is now tugging at her arm. She stumbles after him, leaving behind a shy, backwards smile such as one might give a parent nervously seeing their daughter off on a first date.

Pablo leads the way down winding steps, past beds of cacti, until eventually they reach a lookout point jutting out over the rocky drop below. For a while they gaze out at the sea and sip wine—Pablo has brought with him the whole half-bottle. Jax feels content, partly because of the food and wine, and partly because of the view of water. There's something about water that makes Jax feel safe. Even in London she lives only minutes from the river, on reclaimed marshland—proper riverside accommodation being either screamingly expensive or a slum. In Venice, city of The Engagement, Jonty had insisted they hang out in places like Harry's Bar; the write-up in his filofax had been ringed in biro. Jax had preferred to stand on ornate bridges and soak up the mesmerising kaleidoscopic colours of light playing on the lagoon, watching the water lap peacefully at the riverbank below. In the compromise of Venetian bricks and mortar surrounded by water, Jax saw hope of a contented union with Jonty. Now she imagines that the city's notorious subsidence problem was probably a more appropriate emblem for their relationship.

The setting sun is now casting a salmon wash across the sky. Its colour complements the peachy depths of the dessert wine. Cicadas have started up.

'I hope you like it,' breathes Pablo.

Jax nods.

'But I'm forgetting,' he adds, standing the wine bottle on the ground. Once upright, he reaches into a trouser pocket.

'What are they? They look like under-ripe figs. Or olives. Are they olives?'

'They're a kind of date, we call it a jujube.' Pablo splits the mottled skin of one with a thumbnail and peels it back. Then he dips the yellowish fruit into the wine and holds it out to her lips.

HUNGRY FOR LOVE

Jax hesitates. The gesture feels corny. But so far all Pablo's offerings have thrilled her taste buds and made her crazily hungry for more. She closes her eyes and parts her lips. The intense sweetness of the fruit, which is softer, more fragrant than a date, mingles in her mouth with the wine. Juice dribbles down her chin, which Pablo carefully wipes away.

'Oh dear, my thumb is all wet,' murmurs Pablo, and he brings his fingers up to Jax's lips again. She closes her mouth around them and sucks, gently at first and then more firmly. *Feel your way in.* Quickly he is kissing her, she is kissing him, they are kissing, and an electric shock carries straight to her groin. Pablo tastes of ripe fruit, but with an undertone of something more spicy. For a beat she thinks of Jonty, an automatic reflex, and is almost shocked at how easily she suppresses him. Pablo is now planting greedy little kisses on her neck and she has her hands in his hair, on his neck, on the slope of his shoulders. She pulls him towards her, feeling the enticing swell in his trousers. Then, as with the jujube, Pablo skilfully peels off Jax's clothes, and she his. As they devour each other, the arousing potential of food is no longer in doubt.

MARKET MELANGE

'…isn't all about cooking: creating a lunch or picnic from produce bought at a market can be just as delicious. Markets offer food in season, so most of it will be edible immediately. Make sure to choose contrasting colours and textures, so that the meal, while not home-made, is still enticing…'

The class is gathered outside the hotel. The morning sky is clear and blue although the temperature is fresh. Spiders' webs twinkle on the bushes as though dusted with icing sugar. According to Pablo, an early start is essential to fully appreciate the groaning feast which is the local market.

He appears, wearing olive-green chinos, a thin sweater and a sleeveless quilted gilet. Jax wonders whether he will acknowledge her at all, and so is relieved when he doesn't exactly ignore her but includes her in the general sweep of his welcoming smile.

Conrad was already asleep when she crept in last night, picking the odd pine needle from her buttocks. Pablo is clearly a hungry lover, murmuring sweet nothings at the beginning as if he was saying grace, but with a tenderness of touch that left her senses tingling. Out of his whites he proved to be physically slender and alert, and unhairy everywhere with just a tight tangle of pubic hair against the milky coffee of his skin. His arms and hands were strong and coordinated. She is under no illusion that she is the first, or even the last, pupil to receive such personal instruction. But she exists, can still clearly radiate 'eat me', and last night that knowledge felt important. So much so that she can almost believe that she possesses those fabled pastry-making fingers and skin like cream and, apparently, the moreish insides to rival zabaglione.

On the minibus, Pablo explains about the market and how his father, who was a master baker, used to bring him each Monday to, as Pablo puts it, 'keep me out of mischief'. He makes eye contact with Jax as he finishes this statement and she can almost feel those pine needles from last night digging into her bottom. As the story progresses it is clear that Pablo Senior's form of parental crowd control instilled in his son a lifelong passion for all things edible and it is Pablo's wish that he can similarly inspire others. Jax blushes. Conrad, in the seat next to her, rolls his eyes and lines up another shot of life beyond the window.

The open-air market stalls are all run by men, apart from the rotisserie which is clearly owned by a woman who stands alongside the hot cabinets dressed in a grubby apron. The woman's massive chest puffs out to remind Jax of a farmyard goose up for a fight. Beside her the cabinet is crammed with oiled chickens, already bronzed at this early hour like overeager sunbathers. In passing, Jax breathes in a tempting aroma. The smell of poultry usually creates in Jax a nauseous muscle memory, having once shared rooms with a girl who put chicken bones on to boil to make stock before retiring to bed. The grease from the exploding carcass took up contented residence on the walls of their university bedsit, and never left. If Jax gains nothing more from this cookery trip she will have reclaimed chicken.

Pablo beckons his class around him and talks them through the various stalls on show. The market is designed to be bought from in reverse, in that the stalls at the car-park end sell dessert and cheeses. The idea is to browse idly, inspecting the seasonal produce, but buying nothing, only planning one's menu mentally, on the hoof according to what can be seen and sampled in season. At the far end of the market stand the vegetable stalls laden with fat marrows, bright carrots and dozens of potato varieties. Shoppers can then line their bags with bulbous tubers and other weighty items, before gradually working back to the start of the market, buying protein, herbs, olives and soft fruits before finally making careful room at the top of the bags for the fragile lemon tarts or a punnet of raspberries.

Generosity hums in the air. The men from the stalls urge shoppers to try their wares. Jax is amused to discover that flirting plays its part, but she is eager to try the food more because her own senses are aroused, by the bewitching aroma of rosemary, the gleam of the sliver of goat's cheese or the piece of peach, positioned on the knife and held out seductively, juice dripping down a man's thumb.

Each phase of the market brings a distinctive smell: the pungent globes of cool cheeses, the fresh zing of citrus fruits, or the coal fire of a pancake stall. On closer inspection Jax finds that the pancake is about half a metre in diameter, and is made of chickpea flour. She orders one *socca*, and then studies the vendor swirling thin batter on to the hot pan, black bubbles of trapped air rising and popping, which he presses down with the blade of a large palette knife, releasing yet more charred smells which reach Jax's nose and make her mouth water. When its edges are lacy brown the vendor flips the pancake over and over with his knife into a cornet shape, hooks it out of the pan and slides it on to greaseproof paper. He gestures at a pot of honey but she shakes her head. She wants the unadulterated experience, and almost cannot bear to waste the extra time it would take to drizzle on a topping. He holds it out to her. It feels cosy in her hands. Biting into the crispness her tongue meets the eggy breath of the pleasantly undercooked middle. The vendor laughs at how quickly she gobbles up this most perfect of breakfasts. She leaves a pile of coins and looks around to find the rest of the group.

She rejoins them just as Pablo is showing them how to check for the freshness of fish by examining the scales and the eyes. Jax watches as he massages his fingers firmly, yet gently, over the pearlescent flesh and trembles to recall his touch as he fondled her last night in the dark.

'Penny for them? Isn't that what you guys say?'

Jax jumps. Brian's smile possesses an intriguing complexity. 'You couldn't afford them,' she jokes. Is that so, she thinks she hears him reply, as they both turn back to Pablo and his passions.

He is explaining how he plans his menus and shops for produce. Aromas, apparently, are the secret. Jax thinks back to what Angus the estate agent had suggested about lighting vanilla candles or placing a coffee bean under the grill to make prospective flat buyers weaken. She jots down all Pablo's wisdom in her notebook. Food is about mood, it's about anticipation, it's about temptation, it's about excitement.

'–and there are certain foods that are simply made for each other,' he enthuses. Jax is certain he allows his eyes to settle on her a fraction longer than is necessary. 'Spinach and butter. Smoked fish and cream. Pork and chili.'

And for an hour, the class follows their culinary Pied Piper around the market. At one stall he peels an apple in one thrilling spiral, at another he swiftly joints a quail. There are a few gasps when Pablo snaps the head off an enormous wet fish—Conrad, ever skulking at Jax's side, whispers that he'd just had the same idea—but in the main everyone is carried along in a riot of sniffing, squeezing, finger dipping, note-taking and laughter.

Food is FUN, Jax underlines fiercely in her notebook. Not only can she see possibilities for more than one article, but she is astonished to envisage herself hosting a dinner party, candles aglow, cutlery gleaming, meaty smells wafting around the flat. She and Jonty never entertained in that way. Jonty preferred to host a lively table in happening restaurants—Brazilian-sushi or the temples of gastronomy where the marbled beef rivals the price of gold—and pick up the bill. But now she can imagine herself actually taking something home-made out of the oven. Goodness, it smells divine.

Lunch is back on the hotel terrace. It is draped with vines bulging with fruit, and provides a welcome retreat from the singeing midday sun. Lunch itself is the food they brought back with them from the market. Pablo invited everyone to choose something: a herb, a spice, some poultry or a pudding. And everything blends beautifully, from the pickled jujube Jax chose, with a wry smile, as an appetizer, to Conrad's wild boar sausage and Brian's mild veined cheese. Buying according to the seasons means that all the elements come together, although Pablo throws in some green tea sorbet he made last week, which provides an edgy oriental note and stops the whole thing becoming relentlessly themed.

Jax decides not to drink too much rosé this time round. She wants to be alert for the cooking this afternoon. And

HUNGRY FOR LOVE

there's an hour off after lunch, to compensate for the early start, which she intends to spend lying by the pool.

'God, he loves himself.'

Jax opens her eyes. From her prone position on the sunlounger, Conrad's domed head blocks out the sun. And you don't? she thinks. 'Don't you have ingredients to photograph? Or maybe take a long walk off a short cliff?'

Conrad perches on the adjacent lounger. He is not dressed for sunbathing and Jax briefly wonders why he keeps seeking her out. 'You know your relationship with him is going to collapse like a soufflé.'

Jax sits up and rests on an elbow. 'My relationship? What relationship? With who?' She hopes to goodness Conrad wasn't busy last night practising with his telephoto lens through the bedroom window.

'With *whom*?' corrects Conrad. 'Good job you don't write for a living. Oh wait. You do. Although wait again. You've lost your job.'

Jax sits up properly. 'What are you on about?'

'Look, I know you've been dumped, Jax, but girls with your looks shouldn't go flinging yourself at men—it's pitiful. He's just not, as they say, that into you.'

'Conrad!' Jax seethes. She glances at the pool and sees that the other guests are either relaxing in the chlorine or gazing out to sea. A breeze suggests that they would struggle to eavesdrop. 'Firstly, as I keep telling you, I wasn't dumped. I am the dumper. Secondly, my looks are fine, thank you very much–' she touches her wayward curls, as if to reassure them, 'And thirdly, I am not in a relationship with Pablo–'

MARKET MELANGE

'Pablo? *Pablo*?' Conrad snorts. 'God, no. Why do you mention him? He's way out of your league, I'm afraid. Try the First Amendment's answer to Jamie Oliver. Bumbling Brian.'

'Brian?'

'Cold towel?' The pool attendant radiates an aura that menial tasks are beneath him. Jax and Conrad both take one.

'Why do you mention Brian?' seethes Jax, wiping the chilled cotton around her neck, once the bronzed flunky has sulked away. All the bounce she'd enjoyed from the morning at the market, all that uncomplicated pleasure and potential, has dropped away.

'All I'm saying is, now that you're single, you can use this as an opportunity to find the right man.'

'Crikey—I think I'm mistaking you for someone who cares about me.'

Conrad stands up. 'Ignore me if you like, you know deep down I'm talking sense. Now, I'm off to take some shots of the hotel exterior. Catch you at class.'

As glad as she is that Conrad has walked away, she feels uneasy. Conrad is very precise and task-oriented, whereas Jax's world is one of imaginative prose and creativity. It means that in times of uncertainty there is very little structure keeping her together. When she was told about Jonty's affair with Miranda, she felt as though her brain was wading through treacle. Which, for a writer, is unhelpful. She wasn't sure whether to fight for him, for the sake of the energy and time already invested, or to walk away. The space Jonty left behind was jagged and sharp, and it took all Jax's nerve not to strike some demeaning bargain and sink back into the more cushiony contours of a relationship out of habit.

HUNGRY FOR LOVE

Back then, her mind quickly narrowed its focus to practicalities, confirming the infidelity by checking bank statements and recent email activity. Cancelling the wedding by text was arguably the ultimate practicality. And so here on the sunlounger, to feel proactive again, she turns to her phone. It feels hot from lying in the sun. During the next ten minutes, Jax answers a text from Mike about whether or not she has maimed Conrad yet, and thumbs another to Caryl in which she asks whether Majella has got over the shock.

Suspect you wouldn't want to be any chicken Mum might be currently stuffing, is Caryl's reply.

'Can I join you?'

Jax looks up to find Brian standing beside her lounger. The pattern on his swimming trunks is so zany it is in danger of inducing migraines.

'Sure.' She watches as he lays out his towel, his BlackBerry, his low factor suntan oil, his paperback, his sweat headband, his sunglasses and his flip-flops. All tidy and just so. She recalls the measured way her father drove, something she used to complain about incessantly, in a typical teenage strop. And she can hear his familiar reply: that it was because she was in the car with him that he took such care.

'Hey, those pickled green things you chose for lunch were terrific.'

Brian, she notices, has that slightly overeager manner of Americans consciously out to dispel negative myths about all other Americans. How on earth could we be hated, this frothiness says? Remember us for Halloween and Walt Disney, not for Guantanamo Bay.

MARKET MELANGE

She desperately wants Conrad to be wrong about Brian. She likes that he's friendly. She enjoys male company. But she doesn't feel ready for a relationship.

'Thanks. The market was great fun, wasn't it?'

'Fabulous. Which reminds me–' and he leans down to the side of his lounger and reaches into his bag. 'I bought this for you.'

Jax tenses up. Maybe Conrad is correct. 'For me?'

Brian brings out a slim, dusky bottle with a long neck and a cork stopper. Jax holds it in her hands and makes a stab at translating the label.

'It's a very old wine. Is that what it is?'

'Fifty years old. Used for cooking. I bought it at the market. The grapes are local, matured in sweet oak casks. Try it.'

Jax twists the cork against some residual sticky liquid until it works loose and comes free with a long sensuous pop. The aroma is immediate and makes her mouth water, like some of the loveliest puddings she has ever known. She looks up at Brian.

'Try it. I think you'll like it.'

She holds the bottle at the base of the neck and tilts it gently until a droplet of dark, viscous liquid settles on her fingertip. It sits there proud and shiny in the sunlight. And as her mouth opens to receive it she experiences its smoky sweetness. The taste expands in her mouth and she closes her eyes to drink it all in.

She grins and opens her eyes.

'You liked it!'

'It's amazing.' She turns back to gaze at the bottle. 'Happiness in a bottle.' She glances over at Brian, but his eyes are now closed, his face tipped up to the sun. She can't help remembering that Jonty never bought her anything that wasn't, even in some indirect way, really for him. Even the dresses he paid for were more about impressing the fawning shopgirls than buying something she, Jax, actually wanted to wear. Like baking a complicated pudding for someone on a diet.

Whereas Brian's gift carries genuine thought behind it, bought especially for her. And yet the giver is trying to play it down, which Jax finds pleasantly touching. It's as though she has been given a private blessing.

She looks over at his face lightly dappled with sweat from the humidity. 'So, what do you think of the course so far?'

Brian turns to look at her. 'Great question, Jax. I think Pablo's a genius. A real showman. Did you see him wrestling that cod this morning? Now that's great theatre. I can see him fronting his own show. Can't you?'

A vision of Majella clouds Jax's brain. 'I'm not sure chefs should ever be on TV.'

'You have to be kidding, right? It's what the audience wants today. And that's the first rule of TV. Work out what the audience wants and you'll always strike gold.'

Maybe Brian is in television, or mining and exploration. 'Is that your field? Striking gold?'

'I would've thought that was the goal for everyone, isn't it? To find the secret ingredient?'

Jax holds her breath. Does Brian know the recipe for love? 'For what?'

'For everything. Work, relationships, happiness.'

'Ah, but happiness is elusive. It means different things for different people.'

MARKET MELANGE

'So what does it mean to you, sweet Jax?'

She likes it when Brian slips into courtly language. If he was English, he would have said the adjective ironically, as if it had been mugged by speech marks.

But despite his politeness Jax is stuck for an answer. She is remembering a reply her mother once gave to a Sunday supplement, padding out the issue with quotes from people in the public eye as to what made them happy. Majella's response, even allowing for ruthless editorial trimming, had been succinct: 'happiness was a perfectly risen soufflé'. No mention of her children or husband, the Johnny to her Fanny. Just plain and accurate solipsism. Jax remembers reading the quote and feeling desperately empty.

'Nourishment,' says Jax, surprising herself.

'Hence the cookery course?'

Jax laughs. 'No, I'm here to write this place up for a magazine.'

'Oh what, a show like Oprah?'

'You're obsessed with TV! No, for an old-fashioned thing made out of paper.'

'What, with a contents page?'

'With *page numbers*, and everything!'

Brian has now turned to her, leaning on an elbow. 'And it pays?'

'God no, the pay's shit. But then money famously doesn't buy happiness, does it? Or love.' She thinks of Jonty, her splash-the-cash former fiancé, and about how Brian has interrupted his busy Pilates schedule to take this holiday, peak season. A thought ambushes her. 'I have a horrid feeling you're rather rich.'

'Is that a problem?'

HUNGRY FOR LOVE

'Damn,' says Jax, under her breath. She doesn't want to go through Jonty all over again.

That afternoon they cover pastry and pastas; the following day they look at poultry. By the end of the afternoon, Jax is confident enough to yank off a roasted chicken leg and sink her teeth into its plumpest part. It is the first time Jax has ever successfully cooked herself something to eat which is more demanding than Cup-a-Soup and she is thrilled not just by the juicy tastes but also a sense of pride. She stands at the counter, mesmerized by the tastes and textures on her tongue: the glistening butter, the melting meat, the crisp skin with its burnt bits where the flesh has caught slightly in the pan. Her senses primed by the earlier touching and sniffing, her taste buds are in ecstasy and she chews slowly to delay the moment when the taste must disappear. At one point Jax catches herself thinking about using a peach segment to scoop up a chicken mousse of her own devising and wonders whether she has invented a whole new recipe.

Later, after class, she and Brian share a platonic bowl of almonds on the terrace. The afternoon's tuition majored on stuffing small birds with fruits and nuts, and it has left them with a fit of the giggles. Saggy poultry skin is the running joke of the hour.

Somewhere on the property, a bell is rung, a melodious note, and she and Brian rise for supper. Pablo is serving. Already Jax is luxuriating in the shifting aromas of crisped duck skin, fennel, and a hint of the sea further down the mountain. The complex void of recent weeks, and her in a broken heap at the bottom of it, seems a different life.

96

CELERY SOUP

'…and is therefore light and delicate and yet still tasty. Add a splash of cream just before pureeing for greater depth to your soup, and a dribble of olive oil which will create a smoother finish.'

Caryl opens her front door and presses the communal hall light switch. She wishes she didn't have to, as it only highlights the beige interior beloved of tight landlords. She has fifteen seconds of stark luminosity, accompanied by a loud ticking, to make it to the stairs before being plunged once more into darkness. Barely enough time to check the snowdrift of paper strewn along the warped shelf above a radiator.

Few people actually write to Caryl or indeed to any of the other residents anymore. It's all pizza delivery flyers, random charity tap-ups, and catalogues for lewd yet personalised novelty gifts. For a time Caryl had film DVDs delivered, but it was uncanny how many failed to arrive. The company assured her they had dispatched them, and her bank account had certainly paid for them, but mysteriously they never made it to the hallowed radiator altar. Caryl has always suspected old Mrs. Knight in the ground floor flat, whose television, or should that be DVD player, is permanently on. The only time Caryl bumps into the woman is when Caryl returns from an evening session of Overeaters Anonymous. This is usually at about eleven o'clock because the sessions always overrun, spilling over the appointed time like a bulimic over the toilet bowl. Caryl closes the door soundlessly and yet there stands watchman Knight, tapping her wrist, using her age and slovenly dress sense to intimidate; the boarding house mentality lives on. Caryl has taken to having the DVDs sent to her surgery, where Sue, the receptionist, swoons over George Clooney's abs.

Caryl's flat is as pretty as the entrance to the block is seedy. It's in the eaves—she has achieved this much in her dream to be a writer in a garret—and possesses glorious views out over Battersea Park. If Jax's flat wasn't in a basement, the sisters could lean out of their respective bedroom windows and wave at each other across the Thames. In some sense, by placing herself out of reach, Caryl is hoping that people will make the effort to find her, as her mother might once have bothered to do if her eyes had not been fogged by flour or fame.

Of all people, Caryl knows how fame distorts things. Those regular seasonal features in women's monthlies, *Christmas with Majella*—with the obligatory photo of Jax and Caryl pulling limp crackers—were always shot in August. With the rest of the country basking in scorching temperatures, Jax and Caryl had to don jumpers they had already grown out of, and smile, smile, smile. And once more, for the camera. Caryl hated seeing those photos; even now she cannot bring herself to buy magazines. Back then she would glance at the pictures when the complimentary copies arrived at home, before running upstairs to cry. What she saw was podginess and imperfection, against immaculately styled backdrops. She never considered this image of herself to be a distortion, as false as the scenes themselves. Instead she saw them as a reflection of a deeper, unassailable truth: that she was fat, and useless and therefore unlovable. Why else was Majella's focus purely the stove?

CELERY SOUP

In her kitchen, Caryl makes a chamomile tea. Zero calories. The evening sky is a similar watery hue, the faint wispy clouds like steam. In the fridge waits an elegant hand of organic celery. Digesting celery uses up more calories than are absorbed by eating it.

Sipping tea, she thinks of Jax and wonders how the cookery course is going. Both sisters had collapsed into giggles at the idea of Jax cooking. Caryl is the one who has inherited a dollop of Majella's talent. But she doesn't enjoy it. She will work herself into a frenzy, whizzing round Sainsbury's in her lunch hour and returning to the surgery laden with orange carrier bags. Sue, an unmarried cat lover, once speculated that Caryl must be having a dozen people round for supper, such was the quantity of food bought; and Caryl found herself pretending that this was indeed the case, even though her one bedroom flat is barely large enough to swing one of Sue's pampered Russian Blues. Sue marvels even now at Caryl's long list of otherwise imaginary friends and their hearty appetites, when really Caryl is slinking home of an evening to make flamiche or risotto or brownies or roast chicken and eating it all on her own and then throwing it all up again. Her throat is permanently sore, her teeth a dentist's birthday due to all the stomach acid corroding the enamel, and she hates herself. But for one brief moment, in the adrenalin rush of vomiting, this compulsive inversion of the nourishing process, Caryl experiences the exquisitely soothing balm of release.

Caryl sips her herbal brew. Out in the direction of the sinking sun a plane is making its way towards Heathrow. Who knows, it might have come from where Jax is currently *having fun time, miss you x* with Brian or Pablo or Conrad or whoever. Jax has put herself in this abundant position by being decisive. She has called off her wedding, dumped the fiancé and started life again. She has seized the day, taken destiny by the scruff of the neck, and tossed it into the skip along with all the other clichés. Caryl can only admire her little sister, starting out on her path of finding precious meaning. However, the price of that admiration is also a lingering self-hatred for being such a wimp.

There are no cakes left in the cake tins, and a dose of summer flu sweeping through the local primary schools kept her in the surgery over lunch when she might otherwise have gone shopping. There's the celery, of course, green and crisp and cold from the fridge. Caryl snaps several sticks from the bulb and rinses them under the tap, her thumb cleaning their intimate grooves free of superior organic soil. They rest on the chopping board, wet and glinting in the last of the day's sun.

Caryl opens a drawer and selects a knife. The weight of it in her hand feels reassuring, as if it could cut much more than just vegetables. It's the middle sized one of a set of three, with a black sculptured handle and a fine blade, a housewarming present from Majella, made in Germany. It screams Teutonic efficiency.

OYSTERS

'…and of course they are also said to resemble the female genitalia. This is thought to be behind the idea that oysters are an aphrodisiac, although this is more likely to be due to their high zinc content, since zinc is also good for producing testosterone…'

Jax wakes but keeps her eyes closed. Beyond the room, birds gently herald the dawn. Somewhere to the right of her come the muffled sounds of contented snores. Her lower limbs are aching sweetly, from joggings horizontal now as well as vertical. These past few days she has found herself slowly being unpeeled, in more ways than one. It is a most enjoyable sensation, in the right culinary hands.

Lying there, she thinks back to dinner last night. It had been a meal to arouse the senses. Soft baby squid, delicately fried in the lightest of batters and teamed with a sharp lemon salsa, followed by a soupy rice dish spiked with herbs and flakes of chili. Then duck roasted with fennel, before another of Pablo's seductive puddings which alternated layers of alcohol-soaked sponge, fresh apricots and lavender cream. But instead of feeling lethargic after such a large meal, Jax had felt energised, rampant even, as if Pablo had intended the dishes as subtle aphrodisiacs. After the meal he could be found flitting from table to table, accepting compliments, teasing his class of adoring pupils, and generally flirting liberally as one might scatter hundreds and thousands. People swapped glances, and anecdotes, and then glasses of wine, and finally seats. And so it wasn't long before Jax felt a firm hand on her thigh under the table.

101

HUNGRY FOR LOVE

Jax, lying in her rumpled sheets, dreamily recalls the past few hours. Events may have moved quickly, but they have proved remarkably fulfilling, lacking the traditionally degrading emptiness of a fast food sexual takeaway. From the moment she felt manual pressure on her quadricep, she felt passion ripple through her, a craving which was matched by his.

Once in his room, they tucked in. He began by nibbling her ankles and she felt herself start to simmer, like a pan of milk on a low flame. In the heat of the bed, her very own bain-marie, she bubbled away, as his mouth took him higher up her legs and wave upon wave of desire flowed through her body, feeling that the simmer was about to come to the boil; before his change of pace brought her back once more to a gentle quiver, and the tempting process began again, until at one glorious moment he entered her firmly, whisking first briskly and then agonizingly slowly, until gradually, before she came, she had become as taut as pasta being teased out of a machine, her body long and lithe, stretched exquisitely to the point of ecstasy before being basted in creamy juices and left to relax.

Later, they decided that sex had made them hungry so they raided the mini-bar and gorged on nutty chocolate along with an apple from the fruit bowl. But this was clearly not enough, for soon they could be found gnawing on each other. Or they had become each other's commis chef, encouraging each other verbally as though rooting around for truffles: 'Oh yes! There!', 'Yes! And again!' Taking each other in hand they showed each other what to do, what to knead, what to fondle, what to savour. At one point Jax felt a sharp pain when he bit her nipple, and she cuffed him, but

OYSTERS

was quickly consumed by her own lust, swinging herself on top of him, plunging down on something now the size of a rolling pin, leaning forward for deeper penetration, and tasting his salty sweat where it gathered in shiny rivulets at the base of his neck, blended with traces of peach juice.

Jax smiles to recall the past few hours of happy sex. She can see now that sex with Jonty had become something the *Financial Times* might drily report, with things going up and down like shares or corporate takeover ambitions. Last night instead, for all its sheet-ripping frenzy, felt really quite wholesome. It was as if they had both found in the other some vital ingredient. She feels an urge to run marathons, climb mountains and embrace life's possibilities.

From somewhere in Jax's handbag, her mobile phone emits a tender beep; things happened so quickly last night she obviously forgot to switch it off.

She turns and takes in the other prone body lying in the room. The beep hasn't woken him and he doesn't stir, probably from transatlantic exhaustion! Yes, she has had sex with men before, and recognizes the current post-coital afterglow, but really what lingers is how last night was such enormous squelchy fun. All Sex Features editors on magazines—even Judith, *Your Day*'s agony aunt, who (unintentionally) has been celibate for seven years—agree that in theory, sex between consenting adults should above all be a laugh. The shortest distance between two people is a smile. In practice, Jax has found in the past that baring your wobbly bits to other people can burst the bubble. And certainly Jonty's formulaic tendencies allowed little scope for spontaneity. But now she knows Judith is definitely on to something.

HUNGRY FOR LOVE

And yes, maybe by having lots of sex so soon after ejecting her fiancé, Jax might be said to be morally suspect. But right now she feels a spring in her step having had such a casually fabulous time.

Jax's face is beaming as she pads into the bathroom to listen to her voicemails.

INVALID FOOD

'...when digestion and appetite are poor. Food therefore should be stimulating to look at, enticing, and in small portions so that invalids do not feel overwhelmed. Rich food which is hard to digest is not advisable, but food rich in nutrients and vitamins is essential.'

Jax hurtles down the corridor. At the nurses' station, a woman is measuring liquid into a crimped paper cup, before handing it to a lanky man in pyjamas. On a chair beside the station sits another woman. She stares at her shoes—hunched into herself—unaware that Jax has spotted her. This woman wears no make-up and is sensibly dressed. It is self-effacing women like Sue who keep certain cobwebbed corners of Marks and Spencer's financially solvent. Jax has met Sue a few times and today especially is grateful to see the familiar face. Without Sue, Jax wouldn't be at the hospital at all, but in *Knife Skills: a masterclass* instead. Which is ironic.

'Sue,' Jax calls out and the woman looks up. A smile creases her tired face.

'You got my voicemails.' She stands and they embrace awkwardly. 'And you're here,' adds Sue, retrieving a hankie from up her sleeve and dabbing at her rapidly reddening nose.

'Of course. And my mother?'

'No reply, I'm afraid. I expect she's on her way, though.'

Jax's heart stings at Sue's eternal good nature. Sue expects Majella to come because Majella is a mother, and that's what mothers do. Majella the celebrated cook, with all the implications of nurture and nourishment, who consumes public love like a wild dog around a warthog. Jax feels a flash of anger that even though she has had to jet in from overseas she has still beaten Majella to the hospital. And yet Majella manages somehow to be the person everyone talks about, even when she isn't there. Which only makes Jax more angry. She's damned if she's going to give her mother another thought.

'But where's Caryl? What happened? Is she going to be OK?'

Sue's voicemail messages had been typically efficient, the bare bones of the story. Every time Jax had tearfully listened to it on her journey from the hotel to the airport, and then from the airport to the hospital, she had recalled her own recent succinct nuptial cancellation and wondered at the power of so few words to change the world. The modern equivalent of telegrams from the battlefield.

Sue tucks her hankie up her sleeve. 'I popped round last night to drop off some DVDs. Caryl is so good, letting me borrow them, and I'd meant to hand them over at the surgery, but I forgot. Caryl told me she was planning to be at home, and she is nothing if not reliable. And in any case, I could see her lights were on. But when I got no reply, an elderly neighbour let me in. We– We–' Sue reaches for the hankie again, and Jax puts a hand on her shoulder. Sue looks up. 'Are you sure you want to hear this?'

Jax nods slowly. Which is a lie, because what she really wants to do is run around screaming and turn back time, to when Caryl was well. On some level she doesn't want to hear what Sue has to say—what she hears now can never be unheard—and yet at the same time she wants to know absolutely everything, to feel closer to Caryl.

INVALID FOOD

'We found her lying in the kitchen. The knife was still in her hand. Maybe she fainted–'

Sue sobs quietly into her handkerchief and tired Jax slumps in her chair, feeling overwhelmed by a mixture of panic and helplessness. It's hard to take in that Caryl has tried to kill herself. Caryl, her dear, dear Caryl. The potential finality of it makes Jax's heart quicken. Caryl has always been there, older, wiser, the first of the two of them to use proper cutlery. She thinks, if Caryl goes I shall have no one.

'Can I help you?' asks a senior nurse newly at Jax's side. Jax can hear the neat handwriting in the clear voice; no illegible prescription mistakes will be tolerated on my watch.

'My sister. Caryl. Can we see her? Is she OK?'

'Of course you can.' The senior nurse wears a badge which says Alison. She pauses at the door to smear antiseptic gel around her hands, nodding at them to do the same. Then she leads the way into the Intensive Care Unit. It is only then that Jax realises that her second question has gone unanswered.

The other nurses in the room look up as the three women enter. Glances are exchanged between the staff as carefully as if handling organs for transplant. Jax feels the space of the unit close in on her, as if all the purpose in the room has narrowed down to this one point, this one objective: to heal.

Caryl lies in the bed, as though becalmed. An intravenous drip is hooked into the top of her hand which has begun to bruise. Jax is immediately overwhelmed again, by feelings of sadness and love. Her sister looks so sallow, so frail, so cold. She vows to hold Caryl tight, to warm her up, to never let her go.

HUNGRY FOR LOVE

The mood in the unit is formal, the lighting somehow dim and bright at the same time, and Jax approaches the bed cautiously. Caryl's wrists sport thick pads of bandage, giant sweatbands which exaggerate the emaciation. Jax turns to nurse Alison.

'Will she–? Is she–?' Her jaw refuses to unclench.

Alison places a hand on Jax's arm. 'We've sedated her a little. She was very distressed when they brought her in. Crying. I'll give you two a couple of minutes.'

Jax looks down at her sister. She can't believe she has been so selfish, so preoccupied with her own life and its pathetic little dramas, while her sister has obviously been so unhappy. With a crochet-style blanket draped limply over the slight frame of her person, Jax can see how thin her sister has become of late. Tears well up from her chest and her jaw tightens. I'd do anything to help you right now, my darling girl.

Jax sits gingerly on the edge of the bed. Flat on her back, Caryl's immobile expression resembles shock. And Jax has a sudden memory of a childhood holiday by the sea, Bognor probably, and of Majella buying punnets of cockles and whelks. The vinegar they were doused in made Jax cough. Jax, Majella and Desmond teased out the flesh with pins and ate them one by one; Caryl dug hers out and piled them up on a plate to eat in one go. But just before she could do so, Majella's hand had swooped in like a hawk and grabbed the shellfish and tipped them into her mouth. Caryl's startled face could barely register the parental betrayal.

Jax squeezes her sister's hand. Caryl's eyes flutter open. She takes a while to focus and then Jax sees recognition flit across her sister's features.

INVALID FOOD

'I love you,' whispers Jax, moving closer along the bed.

Still the eyelids flutter, as if Caryl is trying to compute Jax's phrase. She opens her mouth a fraction, her lips cracked and bloodless. This close to her sister, Jax can feel Caryl's lungs struggling to muster enough air to exhale speech. Her head lifts ever so slightly off the pillow.

'Love–' begins Caryl, before closing her eyes again, sinking her head back down again. It's as if the word is too big, too important to utter, thinks Jax. Or too complicated, too exhausting to fathom.

Jax feels a slight tug near her elbow, and understands that she is being encouraged to move away from the bed and out of the unit.

'We need to take a psychiatric history as part of our evaluation. We need to get a sense of how ill Caryl is.'

'Ill?' Jax glances at Sue. For a daft moment Jax thinks Alison means contagious, and wonders if there's been an outbreak of bubonic plague at the surgery that she has yet to hear about—even though it is a talisman held dear by the nation that its GPs are miraculously immune from disease. 'I thought she was just a bit sad.'

'Caryl is seriously underweight, and her teeth show enamel loss commensurate with repeated vomiting. It's important that we build up a profile, that we try to understand what made her cut her wrists. So that we can make the best provision for her.'

'What do you mean?' Twenty-four hours ago, thinks Jax, I was learning how to play with food, unleashing my inner child and stuffing lemons up chickens' bottoms. I have had sex with two different men. I am not ready to play the grown-up and consign my sister to a mental hospital.

HUNGRY FOR LOVE

'Has anything significant happened within the last week?'

'You mean apart from this?' says Jax, spikily.

Nurse Alison nods, patiently. 'A loss, a trauma?'

Jax pauses. Surely this can't be relevant. 'Well, I did cancel my wedding last Saturday–'

'You cancelled it on Saturday or the wedding was supposed to be Saturday?'

Jax wrinkles her nose. Funny how telling Brian this information had been so effortless. 'Both, actually.'

'You cancelled it *on the day*?' A flicker of a smile suggests Nurse Alison is quietly impressed, would actually love to know the details. But quickly a certain medical professionalism kicks in. 'And how did Caryl react, do you know? Did you tell her in advance?'

'Not really–'

'Not really?'

'She knew I'd call it off. That I was unhappy.'

'That *you* were unhappy?'

Jax nods. 'That I'd been unhappy for a few weeks.'

The nurse makes a note. 'Because?'

Jax takes a deep breath. 'And this information will help you help my sister?'

The nurse holds her gaze and solemnly nods.

Jax exhales. 'Because Caryl told me the thing which had made me unhappy.'

'And you were cross with her?'

'No,' wails Jax, tears threatening to spill down her face at the very idea; she could never be cross with Caryl. 'No. Not at all. It's just that she shouldn't have told me. Do you think that's why she cut herself?' Jax suddenly feels very small, as if both she and Caryl have been caught eating sweets between meals.

'I don't know,' says Alison, kindly. 'What did your sister tell you? Why wasn't she meant to tell you?'

Jax, despite not having an intimate acquaintance with the issues of confidentiality in therapeutic encounters, is dimly aware that what she is about to do is unethical, on a number of counts. She glances at the unit, where Caryl's chunkily bandaged wrists speak eloquently of an internal sort of struggle. Do not let my struggle be in vain, they say.

'That my fiancé, my *ex*-fiancé, was having an affair.'

'And Caryl knew this how?'

'She knew the woman. Well, not personally. Well, yes, personally. That is to say, the woman was in her food group. Bulimics Anonymous. I guess I probably shouldn't know that. Or you, for that matter.'

The nurse shrugs, as if to say, it's not my place to say. 'So, it could be a guilt thing? Is Caryl the type to carry guilt?'

Guilt, thinks Jax. Daughter of Majella. Majella, author of *100 Ways with Leftovers*, who has the knack of making your guilt last longer than the Christmas turkey. If Caryl has been storing up guilt for the lean times, then it has been at the expense of calories.

The thought of Caryl's slashed, thin body makes Jax feel queasy. They were born of the one flesh and now Caryl has tried to sever the connection as thoroughly as that first cut of the umbilical cord. She turns to look back at her sister, at the bruises on her hand, at the arm where veins have been sought by increasingly worried medical staff. Her heart knocks against her ribs as she remembers her sister hugging her before Jax left Majella's house and sent the text, when really Caryl was the one in need of the hug.

'So, has your sister always had issues with food?'

Jax spins back round and an uneasy laugh emerges from her throat, the kind of laugh which turns into a cough. 'We all have issues with food. Our mother's a food writer.'

'Ah,' says the nurse, glancing at Caryl's surname on the notes, the penny dropping. 'So, tell me: how would you describe your sister's relationship with your mother, exactly?'

Baking

'…which is why—if I can be technical here for a moment—you must never open the oven door before a cake is done, otherwise the carefully-composed molecular structure of butter fat, flour and egg will simply collapse.'

Dan can feel the letter burning a hole in his apron pocket. He takes it out and stuffs it in a cutlery drawer beside the sink. Think. Think. It's what he was trained to do with bombs, to think ahead. But this is new territory. He doesn't know how to respond.

He retrieves the letter from the drawer, rapidly scans the kitchen—bread bin, flour jar, industrial sized fridge—before restoring the epistolary bomb to the safety of his apron pocket.

STOCK

'...and a good stock can take at least twenty-four hours to make. But there is nothing which adds more depth to a dish than a base which itself is the result of fine ingredients blended with care and judicious seasoning, which makes the time taken to make it the more worthwhile.'

Majella is walking in sensible shoes out of South Kensington station. At the top of the steps she passes a cheery cookie shop, but shop-bought produce is not for her. A commuter makes eye contact and nods at her before heading off to convey, in that reserved yet still starstruck way the British have, that Majella has been noticed—nay, recognised.

Majella walks towards the Fulham Road, passing a vibrant deli-diner in which boxes of panattone swing from every rafter. Majella is reminded of a spat—a while back, in the broadsheets—between her and another television chef (not on a major terrestrial channel, it must be said) who tried to claim he'd been the first to think of using panettone to update the tired British staple of bread and butter pudding. Briskly, unconsciously, she wipes her hands, recalling the victory. Food is Majella's life, the control of it her way of being. Without food Majella would simply cease to exist. It provides her motivation and her relationship to the outside world. Without it, she would fade from the nation's consciousness, or at least its tabloid newspapers. And that really would be death.

She reaches the Fulham Road, where wedding dress boutiques jostle with antique dealers. Without foodie shops to distract her, Majella is reminded of her eldest daughter,

STOCK

lying in hospital, sedated they say, trying to recover from a wound. At first, when Sue rang last night, Majella had had trouble understanding what had actually happened. She assumed her child had had an accident whilst chopping something—easily done when you cook less than Majella does—and the idea almost causes Majella pain. A child of hers, unskilled in the kitchen. It really is incomprehensible.

And then as Sue twittered on, she remembered that it was Caryl who'd had the accident, not Jax. Jax, who has finally seen the light and enrolled on a cookery course. Majella still feels a spasm of resentment, that Jax has willingly submitted to the tuition of a stranger when she has had a lifetime to learn at the master's feet. But Majella has consoled herself with the fact that Jax won't learn much in a week. After that, Majella can nobly pick up the slack.

And the idea pops into her head of a new book, *Cooking for Dummies*, possibly accompanied by a TV series—with a John Lewis tie-in of basic yet tasteful cookery equipment—and she is away: how to boil eggs, make toast, cook spaghetti. If anyone can open cans with chutzpah, it's Majella.

So she is smiling as she walks into the hospital. She still has another book inside her after all, thank God, after next week's fanfare twenty-fifth anniversary reissue of *Food of Love*. Copies have been sealed in cellophane not just to heighten the food-porn elements of the photography but to keep safe one lucky ticket to a day's cookery lesson with Majella, which she hopes to postpone indefinitely by flagging up future writing commitments.

Still, it's a splendid looking book. In her mind she sees the latest proofs, the photos of her recipes as tempting as when she and Parkin were gazing at them in bed last week.

HUNGRY FOR LOVE

She does not see around her the folk in wheelchairs, nor the bald teenager with a mobile plasma stand at his side. She strides to the lifts, presses the button and rides to the top floor, checking her reflection in the mirrored walls, turning slightly to give them her best, her camera side.

As one lift containing a mother ascends, another with her daughter in it descends. In transportation as in life.

ANGEL FOOD CAKE

'…and it's the lightness of the tall sponge which gives this cake its name. Most of the airiness comes from well-beaten egg whites added to the batter. Delicate in colour, this cake works well with summer fruits and a thin glaze for icing…'

'I've ordered you a chocolate velvet cupcake,' says Jax, placing two mugs on the table. 'Hope that's OK. They're the house speciality.'

'Lovely,' says Sue, with an attempt at a smile.

In silence they inhale the fragrant compost of herbal tea. Each is lost in their own thoughts: Sue berates herself for not thinking to take something warm for Caryl to wear in bed, while Jax's stomach is still in knots to recall how she found it impossible to speak when the nurse asked her to describe Caryl's relationship with Majella. It was a simple question and yet the answer seemed so complex that Jax had found herself turning on her heels, walking out of the Intensive Care Unit, swiping her suitcase from the nursing station, and striding to the lift, with Sue calling out after her: 'wait for me'.

Jax pulls up a stool and absently strokes the familiar bare brick of the Barracks Bakery. Behind her the bell of the main door constantly tinkles. It isn't just signalling arrivals, it's like various proclamations of being. And she's reminded of the bells worn by the sheep—or were they goats?—as a way to be found. She can feel her shoulders unknotting. Being in the Barracks Bakery is like coming home.

Dan, wearing his camouflage-print apron, approaches their table. Silently he places before them their order with all the

117

reverence of the Magi before the Lord. Pastry forks gleam at the side, with Dan's thumb holding them just so. Jax's cupcake is, naturally, a cappuccino; Dan didn't even need to be told, he could tell by Jax's worn expression when she came in.

Seeing her unexpectedly here—again!—has lifted his spirits. It's been a hellish week. The army was never like this. Smiling at customers when your world is falling apart is hard and upsetting, and only giving his battered trainers a good workout each morning has stabilised his soul. That and Jax walking through the door, not five minutes ago.

His culinary gifts bestowed, he hesitates and studies Jax's face. It is lightly tanned from her brief trip abroad, her skin bathed in buttery sunlight through the window, and flushed a little from the steam of the tea.

Jax, her head swirling with thoughts of Caryl and Majella, is not aware of Dan gazing at her as though she is made of stained glass. She is staring instead at the coffee icing, like all the secrets of the world might be found there. She cannot know that Dan is pleased with this particular cupcake. That he chose it specially, a slightly larger one than all the rest, and placed the real coffee bean—Jax's brilliant suggestion last Saturday, which Dan immediately adopted—on the peak of the corrugated swirls himself. Just for Jax.

At which point, Dan has an idea to mix meringue with cream cheese frosting to top an ethereal pale sponge with a lemon curd centre; and maybe making angels' wings out of spun sugar, slid at an angle into the icing to shimmer and delight. He imagines placing it before Jax, his muse. He takes one last grateful look at the caffeine decoration, the product of Jax's wise counsel, and backs discreetly away from the table.

Sensing the movement, Jax comes to and is aware simply of the scent of vanilla and spice that Dan has left behind.

'What lovely looking cakes,' says Sue. Everything in Sue's life is lovely. Except that it isn't.

'I know,' says Jax, wistfully. 'This is my favourite cafe in the whole of London. Perhaps anywhere. Dan's baking is simply perfection.'

And both women stare down at their plated treats, wondering why the world has to be more complicated than cake. Cakes which—as Jax knows, having written countless pieces on them for *Your Day*—have for so long symbolised happiness or harmony, which hold deep symbolic or ceremonial significance, and which provide such pleasure in both the making and consuming.

The irony of them eating while Caryl wastes away from malnutrition hangs between them like garlic breath. In their own way, each has found Caryl's attempt at self-obliteration difficult to grasp. It has undermined their faith in battling on, making the best of things. You are perhaps either a cupcake-half-nibbled or half-a-cupcake-left-to-enjoy type person, and it is always destabilising to encounter someone of an opposite persuasion.

'These pretty things take me back to when I was small, and I used to help my mother make butterfly cakes,' says Sue. 'Out of a packet, mind. For God's sake don't tell your mother.'

I tell my mother nothing, thinks Jax. 'Cupcakes are quite the fashion now.'

HUNGRY FOR LOVE

'Are they?' says Sue, eyes wide, as if she has just been told her cake contains cocaine.

'It's a nostalgia thing. Retro. A throwback to when women would make frivolous things after the war, after rationing.'

'Maybe we just want to go back to childhood. Licking the spoon!'

'Except we rarely cook. We come to cafes and buy our nostalgia instead.'

Sue thinks for a moment. 'We're always buying stuff, aren't we? Some of the girls who come to the surgery, not a penny to their name. But always with the latest bag, the latest jacket.'

Jax nods. 'We buy in our comfort.' She sips her tea. And, for a brief moment, watching the summer sun on the bare brick walls, she's reminded that she can now cook, after a fashion. She has sampled her own creations, and they were astonishingly edible! Maybe soon she should try and bake a cake. She'll bake one for Caryl. And for a brief, joyful moment she is thrilled to think of something she can do for her sister until she remembers that Caryl is unlikely to want a crumb of it. Her heart aches.

As if reading her thoughts, Sue shakes her head. 'Caryl's always making cakes. Brings them to the surgery for us all to share, but never eats them herself. Isn't that sad?'

They eye their cupcakes with the same thought: who on earth could resist such unsubtle temptation. The thought of a life without cake is enough to put Jax off her recent ruminations on being a sheep, or a goat. She can almost feel the orgy of buttery crumb melting on her tongue. And in unison they grab their respective cakes and bite in. Their eyes meet and they hoot with laughter.

ANGEL FOOD CAKE

'A moment on the lips–'

Jax shakes her head. 'A little of what you fancy–'

'Oh, my word.' Sue closes her eyes for a moment. 'This cake– It's–'

'I know,' says Jax, swallowing. 'It's beyond words.'

'You've got icing on your nose,' laughs Sue.

'Have I? You, too!' Jax's eyes are watering.

They are now both helpless with mirth, the hysteria masking the memory of Caryl, so bruised and sallow and still. Jax ends up snorting cupcake out through her nose, which sets them both off again. 'I've got a stitch,' groans Jax.

Dan, from his position behind his wooden counter, watches the two of them. His cakes, he knows, have worked their mystical healing again. And not just because of the private blessing he made over Jax's plate before bringing it over. It's a reassuring end to a ghastly week. If everything else fails, he must remember this moment, this quiet achievement. But then, that won't be hard: Dan always remembers the times Jax has been in.

He remembers the way sunlight catches on her eyelashes when she sits near the window with her hands around a mug of tea. Or the way her nose in winter is always red at the tip, beneath the woollen beanie hat she wears pulled down over her ears. She comes, he knows, to cheer herself up and it always seems to work. But this past week, alongside everything else that's been going on, a new thought has begun to bother him. Now that she doesn't have that prick of a fiancé in her life, causing complications, might she start coming less frequently? And if the worse were to happen, and the cafe were to close, would he lose contact with her altogether? Where once he felt safe in the routine and structure of army life, baking is what he knows now, what he trusts, its peculiar scientific alchemy precise yet miraculous. If only one of his own cakes would work some magic, just for him.

THE LARDER

'...so it helps to have cupboards which are well stocked with essentials so that if necessary you can make a meal with no notice, or add personality and an individual touch to existing recipes. Basics such as dried pasta or flour can sit alongside herbs, Tabasco sauce or coconut milk to ring the changes...'

When Jax and her suitcase finally approach the gate in the railings to her flat, she senses the dark shape of someone hovering outside her front door. She shivers, fearing Jonty might have set up camp among the pigeons. She is about to retrace her steps when a fruity voice calls up from the area below. 'Hey, don't break my balls for this one.'

'Brian?' Jax leans over the railings.

'Miss me?' he grins, looking up at her.

She laughs. 'I only left this morning. What on earth are you doing here?'

'You're not angry with me?'

'What for?'

'For stalking you like this.'

Jax laughs. 'Are you stalking me?'

'Sort of. You rushed away without saying goodbye, so here I am.'

'To say goodbye?'

'Well, more like, hello, hopefully. If you'll let me.'

'Well, hello then. But how did you find out where I lived?'

'Well, do you live here? Or just on the pavement up there?'

Jax pushes open the gate and bumps her case down the iron steps. Brian reaches up to take it from her. She had forgotten, in such a brief space of time, how warm is his smile. 'But why are you here? What about Pablo's cookery course?'

'I'd seen all I'd gone to see. But listen, I was worried you'd left because of last night.'

Jax blushes as she fishes in her handbag for the front door key. She remembers the softness of his tongue, as though he had been licking the most exquisite ice cream. And for a moment her shoulders droop with exhaustion. After seeing Caryl in the hospital, the last thing she feels like is having sex. As she worries away at the stiff lock on her front door, she feels an almost panting confusion. She is desperately worried for Caryl, and at the same time longing for the physical warmth of just being held.

She pushes at the door against a minor molehill of post on the doormat.

'Let me help you,' he says, reaching down for the envelopes. He straightens up with them in his large hands and, as their faces meet on a level, her eye is drawn to the V at his throat where last night she had dribbled rosé wine. Barely able to keep her eyes open, she looks up and meets his fond gaze.

'Hey,' Brian whispers. 'You look exhausted. Show me your kitchen, you have a lie down, and I'll fix us something to eat.'

And as she follows Brian into her kitchen, she realises that Jonty would never have judged this moment so well, would not have been capable of understanding how she's feeling, would never even have taken her emotions into account. If Jonty had wanted sex, a shower, a curry, he would have had it. Selfishness personified. It's as if all along she had been planning to marry her mother.

THE LARDER

A minute later and Brian has her laughing.

'Oh my god! Is your fridge always this full?' Brian is standing with one arm wide, the door open to its full extent, in the full beam of an empty fridge. His mortification is only half in jest.

'I've been away. On a cookery course. Meeting naughty men,' laughs Jax.

'But, like, no jars of mustard? No tahini? No tubes of tomato paste? No random garlic cloves? Did you, like, clear out before you left?'

'Maybe I was burgled and the thief was starving?'

'Hey,' says Brian, grabbing another cupboard door. 'Where's the pasta, the pulses? Where are all your "store-cupboard essentials"?'

'My what?'

'I want to cook my English rose the perfect supper but there's nothing here I can use. And I mean nothing. Nada. Your cupboard is bare, Miss Hubbard.'

'You're truly one of the most annoying men I've ever met.' But of course she doesn't mean it. In fact her tiredness is competing with the ripple of excitement that a man actually wants to cook for her. It feels a significant milestone.

She watches while he checks all her cupboards and drawers for utensils and random items of food, feigning a heart attack at the industrial quantities of sacheted soup to make in mugs. He looks more tanned here in the basement flat than he did out in the European sunshine, his Davy Crockett eyes sharp and eager, her 'store-cupboard essentials' as seemingly hard to track down as coyotes.

'Do you do this a lot, bursting in to women's kitchens and critiquing them?'

HUNGRY FOR LOVE

'No, you're the first to experience my Knight in Shining Apron routine.'

And for the first time, she experiences a ruffle of displeasure. After all, a woman who cancels her own wedding by text might be said to possess at least a smidgeon of self-respect. And she wonders, as Brian happily skips round her kitchen, whether she might ever outgrow this rescuing malarkey, this need to be chosen in order to feel valued.

Just as she thinks she might be on to something, a massive yawn overtakes her.

Brian clasps her arms in his hands. 'You sleep, I'll go out and shop. I want to,' he adds, as she starts to demur. 'I take it you know where your nearest supermarket is?'

She tries to give him money, assuming he won't have any sterling, but he opens his wallet to reveal notes in denominations from four continents, rather like his gym memberships. And later, from her bedroom, as she hears him walk up the iron steps to the pavement, she relaxes into the realisation that Brian is someone who is prepared for most eventualities.

Just before drifting off to sleep, she thinks about the various men in her life. Brian is not what you would call a body-god, with his approaching middle-aged folds, but neither is he fat. And she has rather enjoyed having something to get hold of for a change. Jonty is a 'spinning' aficionado—just like Miranda, what a coincidence—and is consequently a hardbody not only in temperament but in physique. Pablo, unlike many chefs, is ultra-wiry, with an obviously fierce metabolism, running on empty even when full. And she is surprised to find herself thinking

THE LARDER

by extension of Dan, he of the astonishing biceps and the strawberry blonde eyelashes and theories about the buying patterns of cakes. In a world largely driven by loud, showy people, Dan has always seemed to her to be a rock of discretion and tact. And not for the first time does she wonder what it might be like to lie securely in Dan's freckled arms—although she quickly rejects the fantasy, not least because she suspects that waitress Sonya at the bakery has the hots for Dan and is probably even now dipping her whisk into the company icing.

But with her eyes fluttering to a close, her mind drifting off into sleep, the last thing Jax sees in her mind is the painting of a cupcake which hangs in the window of the Barracks Bakery. A cake on a cake-stand, as though on a pedestal. Waiting to be chosen. For all its passive 'eat me' properties, it occurs to Jax that it looks lonely and hard to reach.

LINGUINE AL GRANCHIO

'...so as long as you have a handy source of fresh crab nearby, it is the perfect combination of a bland pasta base and the zing of chili and garlic pepping up juicy seafood with some oil for added unctuousness.'

Later, nicely rested, a glass of chilled Chablis in hand, Jax leans against one of her underused kitchen cabinets. With a pang of guilt she thinks of Caryl—currently as thin as vermicelli—and decides that in some way she has failed her sister. She should have noticed her unhappiness. Mouth-watering smells float from pans on the cooker as Brian prepares supper. Jax is absolutely starving, and it occurs to her that only once you are shown how to nourish yourself can you begin to nourish others. She vows to be bolder.

Luckily Jax's nearest supermarket turned out to be a flagship branch—who knew?—which sells utensils as well as ingredients. On to a brand new wooden board Brian sieves a pile of flour before creating a shallow hollow. It looks to Jax like a dormant volcano. Into this he tips some beaten egg and then, with a knife, nimbly draws the flour over the egg before using two fingers and a thumb to do the same. Soon, he has a supple dough. He washes his hands in cold water—cold hands make the best dough, he says, as an aside—and then kneads the dough using the heel of his hand, pushing the dough away, flipping the top over, twisting it slightly before repeating the process.

Jax watches mesmerized, the rhythm of it reminding her of parts of their overseas lovemaking. Watching Pablo making pasta on the cookery course had been thrilling for

LINGUINE AL GRANCHIO

the theatre of it, the speed with which he leapt about the kitchen, spinning loops of dough around his head. Here, in the intimacy of her own little flat, the process seems sensual, even more so as she recalls the way Brian had massaged her skin last night, rendering her as pliable as the dough now beneath his hands.

While the dough rests, Brian begins another dish, coating slippery chicken livers in spiced flour and pan frying them in butter. As the fat bubbles, he throws in a handful of torn sage leaves, until the whole sizzling combination sounds like laughter.

'Happy food,' she says.

'You're so right. And these,' he adds, turning up the flame under the pan, 'are at their best when the outsides are a bit burnt but the insides are still pink and mousse-y.'

Which is a bit how Jax feels, watching the cubes of offal shimmy in the heat. I am at the squidgy end of a holiday romance.

Soon the kitchen is filled with the savoury smells of butter and sage. Jax's stomach rumbles. And she is reminded again of last night, when she thought she might come but somehow, unlike the frenetic al fresco coupling with Pablo the night before—quick, tasty, but perhaps on reflection just a little bit too fast-foodish—Brian had skilfully held her on the brink of climax for what seemed like hours, which had made it all the more ripe when she did come. Now he was at it again, tantalizing her taste buds, making her wait.

She watches carefully, in a vague attempt to take mental notes, as he glugs sherry into the fat so that it sizzles, before tossing the livers around in the juice. Then he tips everything onto a plate, scraping out all the crusty bits from the pan, with the butter and sherry blending into a glossy sauce that glistens on the charred flesh. In one hand he holds out the plate of livers and in another a container of cocktail sticks.

The livers melt on Jax's tongue, the spices sing around her mouth, as Brian returns to the pasta, rolling it thinly with a newly purchased rolling pin.

'My mother was Italian,' he says to her at one stage, as if this alone could explain the culinary spell she is under. 'But I can't talk. If I take too long, this stuff will dry out and I'll have to start again.'

She could watch him all night. Maybe this is the appeal of television chefs like Majella, that they are simply visually captivating. They could be tearing up paper and people would still tune in.

Soon Brian is rolling out the pasta to wafer thinness before cutting and beating it into long strands, like a doll's skipping rope. These he tips into a pan of boiling water, whilst in another he melts butter, garlic and chili. When this is bubbling good temperedly on the stove, he cracks a crab of its meat, as crisply as snapping toothpicks. In one final flourish he at the same time drains the linguine, tips the shellfish into the butter, adds the pasta and stirs it all together. Stylish china soup plates Jax has never seen before, let alone noticed go into the oven to warm, are brought out and the linguine *al granchio* is divided, steaming, between the two.

'Can you tear up some coriander for garnish while I light the candles,' Brian says, tossing her a packet of frilly leaves and leaving the room.

She is about to ask how much is 'some coriander'—Majella would dictate to the nearest leaf—when she remembers

LINGUINE AL GRANCHIO

Pablo's instruction just to feel her way in. She seizes a clump and shreds the leaves, feeling their soft oiliness on her fingers, her nose twitching at the strong aromas rising from the bowl. She is reminded of Conrad when he is in major photo styling mode, when everything must look immaculate. And for a moment she misses her colleague; can almost empathize with his minor, if annoying, obsessions.

'You can bring them through when you're ready,' calls Brian.

Jax carries the food to her own little sitting room, where Brian has set up a makeshift table made out of a pile of books. Onto these he has placed candles which he is in the process of lighting.

At which point Jax wonders whether he might be gay.

Still, she loves his mix of the casual and the serious. The food has been respected but not slavishly so. Spoon and fork in hand, Jax twists the linguine and feeds herself greedily. Clumps of pearlescent crabmeat cling to the pasta and, as she scoops tangles of it into her mouth, garlic butter drips down her chin. Chili tingles the tongue, so that by the time her bowl is empty, it is not just her taste buds but her insides which have come alive. She gasps.

Suddenly, Brian is licking butter from her chin. His garlicky fingers slip into her mouth and she sucks on them fiercely. Then running her fingers around the last of the butter in her bowl she slides them into his mouth and feels him tug on them. They kiss, she feeling his mouth warm and spicy from the food. Quickly they undress, hungry for something other than food. Between them, the pile of books collapses until there's just a heap of bent spines and crockery. Kneeling on an old paperback by Dickens, she straddles her chef. Picking up a final slippery strand of pasta from Brian's bowl she lowers it into his mouth. As the last of it disappears she kisses him forcefully.

'I got ice cream for dessert,' says Brian, gasping after the kiss.

'Oh no, this is your dessert,' murmurs Jax.

Even later, Jax lies in bed, listening to Brian potter about in her kitchen. He is making them both a post-coital snack. A pigeon rehearses its dance routines along the sill outside. The sky glimpsed through the top lozenge of the window is a deepening mauve now that the sun has finally set. And, in the absence of noise outside—the more residential parts of central London can be astonishingly quiet at night—her mind wanders.

She remembers how she used to lie in bed at night as a child, listening to Majella clattering in her kitchen, lots of noise and drama, testing recipes or sampling food sent to her by hopeful producers. And Jax would imagine how it might be if her mother were to come into her bedroom to sit on her bed and ask about her day. And since Jax at the time was being teased at school for having a famous mother, she longed for Majella simply to open her arms and hold Jax tight, and whisper that everything would be all right. Not that Jax would have fully believed her, such is the latent cynicism of the pre-teen. But the fantasy was rich in detail—Majella's magnificent breasts would feel plushy and sympathetic, her clothes for once not smelling of food—and very, very much longed for.

Desmond, on the other hand, used to say, as he tucked Jax up each night, 'Come, my friends, tis not too late to seek a newer world'. Jax loved that phrase, loved the elegance of its lilting rhythm. She assumed it meant something straightforward like Time For Bed, where the newer world was the Land of Nod. Later, Jax's English class learned from Mrs Crouch that Tennyson had written his poem after the death of his dearest friend Arthur Hallam, and Jax began to wonder about her father's nightly repetition of a phrase suggesting loss, a certain restlessness and a craving for change. And lying here in her newly rumpled sheets, with a new male friend clattering about in her kitchen, she sees that Desmond was right: that life doesn't stand still but is in a constant state of flux, that moving forward is the only option.

Outside she hears the faintest whirrings of a dustcart. It is loading a wheelie bin on to its cradle, tipping it up and then setting it back down again, empty. This procedure happens at around nine thirty every evening—a perk from living within spitting distance of the Houses of Parliament and the centre of government. Tomorrow the cart will be back again: same process, different rubbish. The perfect metaphor for life. And she lies there, happily stretching her limbs in the sheets. If she were lying not in cotton but in snow, her arms would be forming the wings of angels.

'So, what on earth were you doing on Pablo's course, when clearly you cook so brilliantly?' she says, when Brian returns carrying plates heaped with slices of fresh fruit.

'And what the feck are you doing in bed with my fiancée?' says another voice, belonging to a man slithering around the doorjamb. In one hand this man holds a spare set of Jax's flat keys. His other is free to land a well-timed punch on Brian's jaw. Raspberries and sliced strawberry fly up into the air before they cascade down, smearing the duvet with blotches of red, like multiple bullet wounds.

LOVE RISOTTO

'…and so with such a celebratory event, champagne is substituted here for the normal wine when making the risotto. The taste is more subtle than is found when using a more robust wine, so use less parmesan in the final shaving, and salted butter instead of unsalted for a little extra kick.'

'I thought you were on my honeymoon in the Maldives,' is the first thing Jax can think of to say, after an initial scream.

'And by the look of things it's a good job I'm bloody not,' says Jonty, rubbing his grazed knuckles in mild surprise—who would have thought that another man could possess so much stubble. If he wasn't so confident in his testosterone levels, fair-haired Jonty might develop an inferiority complex compared to one so darkly hirsute.

Brian is rubbing at his chin, keeping his temper in the watchful manner of a man alert to the sense if not the specifics of the given situation.

'For God's sake Jonty. You don't own me anymore.' Jax untangles her bare legs from the smeared linen and stands beside the bed. 'Are you OK?' she adds, turning to Brian.

'Hi, I'm Brian,' says Brian, trying to keep things civilized. Coyotes, he seems to remember being told, should always be spoken to in a low, unemotional tone.

'Feck off, mate.'

The way that the Oirish is currently drowning out the cultivated estuary of Jonty's preferred banker diction tells Jax that her ex-fiancé is, as his grandmother would say, as drunk as a parlour maid. 'Jonty, get out of my flat.'

LOVE RISOTTO

'I only wanted to check how you were getting on, on your own–'

'Thanks Jonty, but–'

'–but I should have guessed. You're not on your own, are you? You've got him. Mr. New Man.' And Jonty lurches towards the knife which Brian had brought in with the fruit and which now lies on the stained duvet, like a stage prop. Jax, who moments earlier had had visions of being stabbed with her own house keys, lets out another shriek.

'Time you went, I think,' says Brian, lunging straight for the fist holding the knife and forcing Jonty to drop it. Then he hauls Jonty towards the bedroom door.

'But I love her,' says Jonty, on the verge of tears, believing in his inebriation that he might connect with Brian, man to man; that he might confess and receive absolution.

Jax sees that Jonty's knuckles are tinged with white as he grips the doorjamb to stop himself being dragged away by Brian. Her heart skips a beat. Is it true? Does he really love her?

'This isn't love, Jonty,' says Brian. 'Whatever you think love is, this isn't it.'

While Brian is up on the street, attempting to hail a black cab—oblivious to the fact that the twin factors of being dressed in a bath-towel while holding a lairy drunk are seriously compromising the success of the mission—Jax is in her kitchen making strong, instant coffee. Not for her the scoops and grinders of Majella's preference. Two teaspoons of freeze-dried granules is as sophisticated as Jax's coffee making gets.

As she waits for the kettle to boil, she thinks about Brian's comment, his apparent certainty, that whatever

HUNGRY FOR LOVE

Jonty's recent behaviour amounts to, it isn't love. Standing here in her bare feet she feels as clueless as ever about the recipe for love. But the word has haunted her, most of her life. Because for as long as Jax can remember, Majella has been asked in interviews what brought her to cooking and her stock reply is that food is love. It became Majella's mantra, her catchphrase, and the title of her original best-seller. And no one could possibly doubt it because to do so would be to doubt the whole concept of mothering. I feed you because I love you.

But as she stirs sugar into her coffee, Jax feels under-skilled in love, which she takes to be a chronic deficiency in adult life. She experiences this now, despite the orgy of food recently eaten for supper, as a yawning gap in her insides, wide and grey and empty, like the pages at *Your Day* before the text is set. Certainly as she was growing up, and Majella was preoccupied with the tremendous triumph of *Food of Love*, and then the planning of the next books, and their successes, and the subsequent celebrity, Jax was aware of some sort of niggling, impossible to articulate discrepancy. She thinks about how no one seemed to care about how it felt to be Majella's daughters—your packed lunch laughed at for its frittatas, your birthday parties invaded by photographers wanting shots not of you, but of the train cake made out of Swiss rolls, when what you'd secretly been hoping for was a cake in the shape of a princess in a ball gown. Jax's throat almost closes up at this memory, and she chokes on her first sip of coffee.

Everyone assumed Majella loved her family because she was such a maternal-looking women and a fabulous cook. That food really did equal love, and that the love was fully reciprocated. That the equation was simple. My mother's cooking has been a way to try and love herself. Through cooking, my mother has hoped to heal a hurt.

Jax blows on her coffee. So love does not come from food, or not explicitly. And Jax is conscious of another thing that love is not. She recalls Jonty, and his infidelity with Miranda. Yes, in some quarters it would be regarded as unethical that she should discover this, but Caryl had been quite clear: she had a duty to protect the sister she loved. Love of one's sister came, for Caryl, higher than confidentiality within The Group. Or as Caryl herself saw it, Miranda had forfeited her right to confidence by betraying the wider sisterhood. At the time, Jax had not given a toss about the ethical niceties. Instinctively she saw that such betrayal was Not Loving, that it was not the kind of thing you did to someone you loved.

So that is what love isn't. It isn't having a secret life and telling lies. Jax knows that much.

But that assessment brings her no clearer to finding her way around love. Did sex with Pablo equal one-night love? Is Brian merely a summer romance? Does Dan love cake more than people? And might Jonty—she almost cannot bear to think this, her hand holding the coffee mug is almost trembling—might Jonty have discovered that he loves her, just in time?

MADELEINES

'...melted butter, which makes for a pure batter, and a delicate flavour for the cakes. This can then offset stronger accompaniments such as stewed fruit or a rich ice-cream. It is fashionable to serve these fancies as part of a dessert, but they can also be dunked in a morning coffee too.'

After the dramas of the night before, Jax and Brian return to bed and sleep late. Technically, Jax is still on leave, supposedly on a cookery course instead of honeymooning on some precarious atoll in the Indian Ocean.

She wakes earlier than Brian—his lower cheek now a mottled purple—and lies in bed listening to the throaty coos of the pigeons who are making a valiant effort to drown out a man in the street disputing his parking ticket.

She cannot decide whether London going about its business is a support or a humiliation. When she became engaged, her life acquired some direction. Even becoming unengaged had at the time felt proactive. But now she is in a state of confusion. If she had known in advance that cancelling her wedding would have unleashed such turmoil—Caryl's overdose, Jonty's violence, her own rather pneumatic sex life—she might have been tempted instead to walk down the aisle.

When Brian wakes he finds her sitting up in bed, her arms hugging her knees. 'Don't worry about Jonty. We can change the locks. He'll never bother you again.'

We can change them? thinks Jax. She feels very weary. Scraping her nails through her hair, she feels the grease and the dirt on her fingers. 'I never told you why I left so abruptly, yesterday morning.'

'No, you didn't.'

'My sister slit her wrists. She's in hospital near here.'

'Oh my Lord. That's, like, awful.'

'I'll be going to see her later.'

'And you want me to come? You don't want me to come?'

Jax half smiles. 'You're right. I don't know.'

He reaches out for her hand. 'Why didn't you say?'

'I don't know. I think I'm in denial. I'm terrified she might die.'

Brian sits up alongside her. 'Look. I loved last night. Maybe not this bit,' he touches his jawline gingerly, and winces, 'but supper and stuff, it was fun. I love that we met on the course. But I'm a big guy. I can take care of myself. I'm not asking to stay here. I've got a place of my own—'

Jax smiles to recall the four gym memberships.

'—but you've got heavy-duty stuff going on. Like, I don't want you to feel like you're on your own here.'

Jax looks at him quizzically.

Brian ticks the issues off on his fingers. 'Well, in the last week you've cancelled your wedding, your sister has tried to kill herself, and your ex has threatened you with a knife. You need some support, is all I'm saying. What about your folks, do they know about any of this?'

Jax runs her tongue around her back teeth. 'My father isn't around anymore.'

'Which means your Mom is?'

Jax nods, aware that by saying nothing she is also saying a very great deal.

HUNGRY FOR LOVE

'So, what do you usually do when you've had a lousy day and the world seems against you?' asks Brian.

Jax watches Brian discreetly, over what he calls the *frosting* of her cupcake. She'd hoped that he would like the Barracks Bakery, that he would appreciate its New York bare brick vibe and manly colours, but she had not expected him to be so utterly gripped. At first, with his transatlantic tan and button-down shirt—his initials are stitched to the pocket in large font—he had looked out of place, a little too big for the zinc stools. But as he casually strokes the tabletops and takes in the unobtrusive camouflage themeing on the napkins and take-home bags she can see he's enthralled. And as he stands at the counter, being talked by Dan through all the various cupcake options, the tray bakes and the specials, which today include courgette popovers and some baby hazelnut bundts, it seems to Jax that Brian is almost hyperventilating.

'Can you believe it, they've got a chocolate loaf made with beetroot,' he tells her, excitedly, as he returns to their table. 'That guy at the counter gave me a sample. It's so moist I bet you could smear it on like body cream.'

Jax slaps him playfully. 'So which one did you go for?'

Brian gives a sort of embarrassed shrug, as the first of fourteen plates arrives at their table. Brian has not, in the strictest sense of the phrase, made a choice at all, not in the sense that choice usually involves a relinquishing of alternatives. He doesn't eat every last crumb—Jax does her best to help him out—but each baked item sampled is clearly savoured and mentally documented.

As he eats, he hardly speaks, and Jax has time to glance up to see what Dan is doing. She is surprised to find him

MADELEINES

looking straight at her. She decides that he is taking pleasure in not only receiving such a large order but also in simply observing a customer's obvious delight.

Dan blinks and realises Jax has caught him staring at her. His Caramac freckles acquire a ruby coating and hurriedly he sweeps non-existent crumbs from the counter. He wants to hate the fact that Jax seems to attract men with wallets of cash, but hate has never really been part of Dan's repertoire. He didn't join the army to kill people, but to save lives. And if the man in question brings Jax to the cafe then Dan is prepared to focus on the upside.

And quickly he has an idea. He starts boxing up some plain miniature madeleines for Caryl. Perhaps these tiny buns might tempt Caryl to break her fast—his layman's understanding about Caryl's emergency hospitalisation being fairly sketchy. But surely no one could resist such dainty fancies? And maybe the hospital staff would like some too? They're probably rushed off their feet and could do with cheering up. And while he's at it, he might as well slip in a couple for Jax as well. And one for the flash bloke in the monogrammed clothes.

FISH SUPPERS

'...and if you only have the energy to slump on the sofa after a day at work, you can still make a fish dish in the time it takes to drink something with ice in it. Depending on its thickness, fish takes just minutes to cook and is the perfect foil for sauces to perk up even the most jaded spirit.'

Your Day's editorial meetings are held during the first week of every month. Each edition is planned four months in advance, so even though it's now July, the edition currently being planned is for November. Which in the peculiar world of magazines, is called December.

The lift door opens and Jax is faced with the sight of an all too familiar office. Colleagues surreptitiously check Facebook and Twitter. When Jax left here last week, she was engaged and about to be married. Now she is stone-cold single. At some stage in recent months she had fantasized about this moment, or at least a variation of this moment, emerging from this very lift, sporting an Indian Ocean tan, to a chorus of envious sighs. Last week, Jax's assistant Chloë—otherwise known by the hair-splitting title of Sub Deputy Chief Sub Editor, the one responsible for collecting wedding list money from colleagues and buying a nest of casserole dishes—had organized an extra little whip-round and bought Jax an Ann Summers garter. This morning, Jax, her feet poised to touch the coffee-stained carpet tiles, wonders whether, like all the other matrimonial gifts, she is expected now to give these items back.

The air in the office smells stale, as if nothing at all, not a plant leaf, not a venetian blind, has moved in her absence. She has no reason to be here, but after the peace of the Barracks Bakery, the sight of Caryl still prone in the unit has tipped Jax off balance again and she has felt the need for something familiar. The medical staff were thrilled with their miniature madeleines and suggested Jax came back around lunchtime when they reckoned Caryl would be, if not hungry, then less sedated and hopefully talkative. Majella, they informed her, had also visited yesterday. Would she be coming again, they wanted to know? It was a question said in such a way as to suggest they were hoping the answer would be no.

Colleagues look up and arrange on their faces expressions of commiseration. To them, a cancelled wedding would herald desolation. Jax feels their pity scratch her skin. Like a child reaching for its favourite soft toy, she reaches in her bag for her mobile phone. Earlier, on leaving Dan's bakery, she and Brian had punched in their respective numbers—does that make me a modern slut, she wonders, for sleeping with someone before knowing their number?—and, for a moment, its numerical presence protects her in the office from feeling helpless. With a final stroke of its casing, Jax smiles at her colleagues, dumps her bag at her desk—tidy in its smug, I'm-Away-on-Honeymoon emptiness—and boots up her computer.

The section heads are already gathered in Mike's office. It's only when she pops her head the door, that she sees the dome of Conrad's sun-kissed cranium.

'The wife returns,' he smirks. 'Or should I say "singleton"?'

'You can say what you like, Conrad,' says Jax, sweetly. 'No one's listening.'

'Children,' scolds Mike, sucking on a nicotine substitute cigarette.

HUNGRY FOR LOVE

'And anyway, what are you doing back so soon? Pablo throw you off the course?'

'The only thing that man can throw is pizza dough,' scoffs Conrad.

'If those of us not fortunate enough to have overseas business trips might be allowed to continue?' says Mike, inhaling deeply. 'Now, the December issue. I'm thinking Partridge In A Pear Tree theming, I'm thinking holly on the pews, I'm thinking mince pie wedding cake. I want tradition with a twist.' He coughs, out of habit. 'Well, obviously I couldn't give a toss, but the readers love it.'

'I could tweak the photos from Jax's wedding,' says Conrad. 'Add a few seasonal touches, frost on the grass, and then—oh! I'm sorry Jax. Me and my big mouth.' He fakes a smile as Jax shoots him a sarcastic look of pity.

'So, how are the ongoing episodes of Life with Brian?' whispers Conrad as the editorial team troop out of Mike's office clutching folders to their chests and deadlines to their hearts.

Jax stops dead. 'How did you know Brian was here?'

Conrad rolls his eyes. 'Duh. Who do you think gave him your address?'

'You? But why? Why so nice, all of a sudden?'

'I thought it might be fun. He's so annoying, isn't he?'

Jax recalls Conrad's comments by the pool. 'You told him where I lived because you think he's annoying? I think you're annoying, but I don't go setting you up on dates.'

'I know,' Conrad smirks. 'You're saving yourself for me.'

Jax rolls her eyes. Yes, the office is the new crèche.

'So tell me, how long before you kicked Brian out?'

FISH SUPPERS

Now it's Jax's turn to smirk.

'Don't tell me he's still there? But he's awful. He eats with his fingers.'

'That's not all he does with his fingers.'

Conrad gags. Jax slides into her seat and starts sketching out her article on post-break-up holidays.

Before lunch, Jax leaves her office and splashes out on a taxi to the hospital. Halfway down the Brompton Road she thinks she sees Majella on a pavement and her heart lurches. She looks away but the temptation to pick at the scab is too strong and she glances back to discover that actually it's a poster of her mother in a bus shelter. It's advertising the new, improved edition of *Food of Love*, with the legendary 'If you can read, you can cook' slogan emblazoned at an angle, being relaunched in all good bookshops and supermarkets, *now!*

That bloody book. Jax would quite happily toss every copy ever printed onto a bonfire and stuff global warming. But now there are to be more! Just as there will be, no doubt, more interviews on breakfast TV sofas, more profiles in the Sundays, more radio sound bites. And it crosses Jax's mind that in spilling the beans, the long-soaked pulses of her life, Majella might also casually mention the devastating news of the cancelled nuptials. After all, Jax's own career at *Your Day* has drummed into her that the secret ingredient in any successful piece of journalism is personal conflict. Anger floods Jax from top to toe, her feet fidgeting in rage. She taps the cab floor so much the driver thinks she is annoyed at the route he's taking, and, out of guilt, he lets her off the entire fare.

HUNGRY FOR LOVE

Waiting at the lifts, Jax still feels angry. Jonty cheated on her and the universe tilted on its axis, so that her confidence drained away. No longer could she expect a relationship to ground her in an uncertain world. Which is clearly, now she thinks about it, what everybody secretly craves. Majella is grounded by her relationship with food. Successful recipes mean order in the kitchen. For Caryl, the relationship is also with food. Food is the thing that can be controlled, even when the urge to eat it hasn't been. Stability out of chaos. It's as old as time.

I'm here, she telegraphs to Caryl as she emerges from the lift into the hushed atmosphere of Intensive Care. She loves Caryl unconditionally, loves her loyalty and her constancy, and hopes it isn't guilt about revealing Jonty's infidelity which has triggered the wrist slitting. Jax's heart flutters: her sister's desire for control has literally reached life-threatening proportions. But at least Caryl isn't hunched over some toilet bowl somewhere. Thank heaven for small mercies. And a faint smile twitches Jax's lips. Black humour. Where would we be without it? The irony of a mother who cooks, a sibling who won't and another who throws up.

AMUSE–BOUCHE

'…which literally means 'mouth amuser'. They are usually the preserve of upscale restaurants, with chefs trying to impress. But as a way of enticing your guests for the meal ahead, unusual ways with smoked salmon or vegetables look impressive yet are easy to pull off…'

'Did madam enjoy?'

Majella dabs her napkin at the side of her mouth. From her corner seat she can view the entire dining room, apart from those tables in restaurant Siberia. Her young guest has his back to the room, even though he'll be the one picking up the tab. He wasn't even asked if he would like to choose the wine, but to be in a restaurant of this calibre, with its sumptuous soft furnishings and bonsai table arrangements is a pleasure in itself, so he isn't complaining. He's lucky, he knows, on his meagre publishing stipend, to be gathering up the crumbs here at all, since this is not a lunch for him but for Majella.

This much is evident from the behaviour of others in the room. The waiter's emollient seeking of Majella's opinion is no mere formality: she was recognised on arrival by the maître d', and this vital information was rapidly relayed to a stressed kitchen already frantic with the early lunch sitting. Complicated amuse-bouches have miraculously found their way to their table, as have frosted glass slates bearing four different flavours of butter.

Majella inclines her head, knowing that many of the staff are furtively watching, waiting for the Bateman Cartoon moment when a well-known cookery personality turns into 'The Woman Who Passed Judgment on a Meal in their Restaurant.' Majella can almost hear the dining room holding its collective breath. It's a moment of exquisite power and Majella will only relinquish it when she's ready.

'The risotto,' she says, and opens her palms, 'was dry.' And she takes a mouthful of wine, as if to suggest that all the rains in England could not slake a thirst caused by a dish so desiccated.

Her companion, Toby, recently promoted publicity manager for *Food of Love*, thinks it can't have been that dry, given how enthusiastically Majella gobbled it up. Greasy takeaways with his sister from the Bamboo Curtain, round the corner from the flat they share—the mortgage is large, their salaries small—have instilled in Toby an ability to eat what is put in front of him without complaint.

The offending empty plate is whisked away and Toby watches Majella glance up, just a fraction, a micro-gesture, to see whether anyone is still watching. This lunch was the idea of Toby's boss, Majella's prematurely grey editor Will, who wants to keep Majella sweet while the publishing house breaks the news to her that the plans for the twenty-fifth anniversary relaunch for *Food of Love* are rapidly unravelling. With two days to go, Will and Toby have discovered to their absolute horror that neither of them confirmed in writing the booking of the venue, a newly-opened private members club, for the party. Yesterday they learned that the location has been commandeered by minor royalty, so Will finds himself grappling not only with the trauma of no venue but with the prospect of being trumped in the following morning's newspaper coverage by perhaps an imperial engagement.

AMUSE-BOUCHE

Toby was supposed to have raised the matter with Majella once the food order had been taken—he and Will have carefully role played this very scenario for the last twenty-four hours—but what with the bread selection and Majella's forthright description as to how the amuse-bouches might have been improved, Toby's courage now resembles the wilted spinach which minutes ago accompanied his roast turbot with paprika aïoli.

'So tell me, Tony, dear. How are the acceptances to my launch party going?'

Majella has no reason to think they are anything other than healthy and rising. Whispers about her tome in the trade press have spoken of cordon bleu production values, fusion photography and mouth-watering prose.

Toby stares at the crumbs being delicately ushered off the linen cloth by a hand wielding something silver which resembles a scalpel. If she calls me Tony once more, he thinks, I shall stab her. Alternatively, if I stabbed myself I wouldn't have to endure Majella's 'dry risotto' countenance. The face beaming from posters which lately have escorted him, at a slight angle and at regular intervals, up the escalators of his daily commute, bears little resemblance to the sour woman with whom he has just spent, he checks his watch, forty-six minutes.

'Somewhere else you have to be, Tony?' she drawls.

Anywhere, Toby thinks. Anywhere but opposite you. And in fantasizing about wrestling the waiter for the scalpel, he wonders whether years of wrist action—pulling out corks, carrying multiple plates—will render the outcome an embarrassing foregone conclusion not in his favour.

Majella also glances at her watch. 'Well, I must be off too,' she announces. 'I have to be at the hospital.'

HUNGRY FOR LOVE

You are ill! Toby inwardly rejoices. You're too ill to make the launch and my mission is irrelevant. I might even stay for pudding. 'Nothing serious, I hope,' he murmurs, in well-drilled publicity tones. And then maybe, he muses, a cigar.

'My daughter. Cut herself,' she answers succinctly, as befits a woman famous for seasoning her food sparingly. And she rises and leaves the dining room, the waiters parting like the soft peaks of whisked egg whites.

And Toby finds himself tempted not just by the chocolate fondant or the praline crème brûlée but by an urge to order both and to pretend on the expenses sheet that Majella stayed to eat one of them.

Yes, thinks Toby. If I was your daughter, I'd probably cut myself too.

SOUR CHERRY TART

'...and the crisp pastry shell is a wonderful contrast to the eggy filling studded with tart fruit. Of course the fruit can be varied according to the season, but this combination of taste sensations is particularly good.'

'You're telling me you've somehow managed to lose the venue for a launch party due to take place in two days' time?'

The voice currently booming around the hospital lobby was once described by a food critic in the *New York Times* as being like someone sharpening knives, badly.

'And no, Toby didn't tell me. Too busy mooning over our waiter, I imagine. What?'

This last is addressed to a man—a porter, in blue antimicrobial fatigues—who with a winning smile and a diploma in prenatal studies from the University of Lagos College of Medicine, but no legal right to be here, wishes politely to point out the sign requesting that there be no mobile phones used on the premises. The graphic is prominent and unmistakable: a handset with a red cross through it. You don't need a degree from any university in the world either to understand or comply with it.

'No, I'm not giving autographs,' Majella snaps at him, and strides towards the lifts.

Two women chatting recognize Majella from all the books, the television shows, the poster in the bus shelter opposite the hospital ('if you can read, you can cook'). They pull faces at each other, and one of them takes a photo on her phone which she then posts on Twitter. She never could get Majella's plum roulade to work properly, so it is healing for her to discover that Majella is actually a grumpy bitch.

Dan is standing in the Barracks Bakery kitchen, beating sugar into butter. The fat wasn't as soft as it should be but, even so, Dan's worked-out muscles on the wooden spoon are a fraction too vigorous. Sonya, today wearing earrings in the shape of tiered cakes, has already told him he should be using the bakery's industrial-sized Magimix which would do the job in twenty seconds. But for now Dan prefers to stand with a brown bowl cupped in the crook of his elbow, whacking the ingredients to a pulp by hand.

'Beat that food any longer and you'll be had up for assault,' says Sonya, nodding at his bowl as she breezes past carrying a fresh batch of chocolate velvet cupcakes. The cafe can never sell enough. Beat me instead, Sonya pleads silently, before wiggling out of the kitchen.

He stares down at the pale amalgam, and reaches for the eggs. Their brown shells remind him of the tanned skin of Jax's hungry friend. It was, thinks Dan, generous of him and his enormous wallet to buy so many cakes, but really. Cupping the bowl in one arm Dan smashes an egg on the side, followed by others, hurling the cracked and empty shells into the bin.

Sonya appears at the door to the kitchen. 'There's a man to see you,' she says.

Dan freezes. For days now, since receiving that letter, Dan has been hoping this moment would never come. Ten years diffusing bombs, and yet in the world of finance he feels at an immense disadvantage. Maybe this is all for the best. I don't have a head for business. I am simply someone who happens to be good with his hands.

But then he remembers that people adore his cakes, that his clients always walk out of his shop with smiles on their faces, that Jax is still frequenting his cafe despite a hellish week involving a cancelled wedding and a sick sister. He must be doing something right.

He puts down the bowl and finds his arm has gone stiff. Cramp. His other hand is covered in egg goo which he wipes down the front of his apron, but then regrets it. A clean apron is a source of pride to Dan and right now, he knows, he needs to make a very good impression.

Jax hears her mother before seeing her, the tart tones emerging from the lift to puncture the hushed bubble of Intensive Care.

Her mouth goes dry. She has not seen Majella in person since the night before what should have been her wedding. Caryl had retired early to her en suite, after a supper of Majella's smoked beetroot gnocchi. Jax was lingering in the lounge, still not entirely sure she had the courage to call the whole thing off. Majella was sat with Parkin on the sofa, stroking her surrogate child, watching television. I've been betrayed, Jax wanted to say out loud, to see whether those hands might be persuaded to reach out and caress a real child for once. For that was how Jax had felt in that moment, very young and afraid of the future.

And she was reminded how once long ago, when she and Desmond were out having ice cream together—Mivvis they were, crammed with forbidden artificial colours, a shop-bought, post-school treat, their secret—Desmond had started talking about The Future as if it was a distant, mysterious land that people visited, but from which they never came back.

'And one day, you'll get married,' he had added.

And Jax had grimaced and said she wouldn't because, even though secretly she hoped to wear a white dress one day, at that stage no boys at school were asking her out and she couldn't bear to contemplate years of invisibility. And Desmond had said that never fear, one fine day he would get to walk her down the aisle. And Jax had stuffed her Mivvi in her mouth and had shaken her head. And Desmond had gazed at his daughter and said that, all right, if one day, in the future, they ever walked down the aisle together for her own wedding and she got to the end and realised at that moment that she didn't want to marry this person, then she only had to turn to Desmond and he would understand completely, take her by the hand and lead her away. And Jax had been left wondering why her father would ever imagine that such an offer might even be necessary.

So on the eve of the wedding, Jax had been on the verge of speaking to Majella, could feel the tide of anxiety, the urge to confess, bubbling up from some deep amniotic level, from some primitive need to be held and understood. Her father would have known what to do, and she felt a soreness in her chest at his absence. She had opened her mouth. And Majella had looked away from the television— Parkin had complacently looked up too, as if the two were in total agreement about this, had perhaps regretfully had to discuss it many times on their walks, before coming to this conclusion—and said, 'Now remember, Jacqueline, don't be late walking down the aisle tomorrow. It's not your day.'

'Turn that phone off now,' barks nurse Alison, sprinting down the corridor. Her shoes squeak on the lino, setting Jax's teeth on edge.

Majella breaks off speaking and looks up. It's been a long time since someone has shouted at her with such authority and she is momentarily reminded of her own mother, in the days before the bolt to Madrid. Jax, following in Alison's wake, has never seen Majella reprimanded before and is struck by the flash of contrition which crosses her mother's face. It disappears just as quickly but Jax knows she definitely glimpsed it and feels in that moment a sense of connection, a hint of that sacred bond that binds parent to child.

The phone is switched off and slipped without further fuss into Majella's handbag.

'The medical equipment. We have to be rigorous about phones. I'm sure you understand.'

'Of course,' murmurs Majella. 'It was just that—'

'I was just saying,' says Alison, hard-working head of the ward and routinely unimpressed by celebrity culture, 'that unfortunately Caryl is not able to receive visitors at the moment. She's very distressed, and has required further sedation.'

'Do you mean some sort of relapse?' asks Jax.

Majella shoots Jax a look, as though Jax is to blame.

'We often find this in cases like Caryl's, when the patient realizes that in fact they've survived. It can be most traumatic for them.'

HUNGRY FOR LOVE

'But I saw her last night,' says Majella. 'She seemed fine then.'

'Well, it's possible that *some* visitors are tiring her out.'

'I hope you don't mean—'

'I mean that your daughter is still unwell.'

Majella looks bemused. What she has taken in is that her daughter has cut herself. 'But in the early days of my career, I was cutting my fingers and thumbs all the time. A good sharp knife, that's what she needs.'

No, thinks Jax. She's already got one of those.

'What she needs,' says Alison firmly, 'is time.'

Majella glances at her watch, as if to signify that she could wait, at a push, another five minutes.

'And understanding,' adds Alison.

Jax remembers that she never did answer Alison's question about the nature of Caryl and Majella's relationship. Probably doesn't need to, now.

'What I'm saying,' says Alison, addressing both women, 'is that I think it's best if you leave, for now. I'll call you if there's any development.'

Majella and Jax look at each other. In their slightly dilated pupils, their blood-drained lips, is the realization that they will be alone together, if only for the duration of a journey in a lift. Neither is relishing the prospect.

When the doors close, they are alone. The scuffed buttons for each floor become immensely fascinating. And unlike fast lifts in hotels in places like Dubai or Shanghai, lifts in hospitals, for the transportation of the sick or infirm, are lethargic to the point of comatose. Bracing herself for a verbal attack about cancelling her wedding, Jax tries to control her breathing, which has become rather frothy. And

SOUR CHERRY TART

yet remembering the fleeting change to Majella's expression just now, Jax is also wondering if this might be her moment to make amends, to appeal to a mother who might after all, behind the poached poultry bosom, have hidden reserves of compassion. The arrival on the second floor of a woman in labour being rushed to theatre puts pay to that little plan.

On the pavement opposite the hospital, Jax realises that Majella, checking her watch, is standing incongruously next to a poster of herself—with its faintly condescending slogan— in one of the bus shelters. One would never guess the two Majellas were even related. One is smiling and suspiciously free of wrinkles. Something about the chestnut tones in the hair suggests she has a warm relationship with food and is selflessly keen to pass on its secrets. She strikes Jax as vibrant and alive, charmed almost, the very essence of wholesome vitality. You just know she'd make a great Mum; Jax would love to meet her. The other is frowning at the world, her maternal qualities thinned out like food for invalids.

'Well, I certainly wasn't expecting to have nothing to do,' says Majella, for whom an empty diary is a personal affront.

'Don't you have stuff to arrange for that?' asks Jax, nodding at the poster.

Majella spins round and confronts the poster before stepping back, as though in horror, and walking away. The cancelled wedding is clearly far from her mind.

Jax wonders whether she should push her luck. 'Do you fancy a cup of tea or something?' she calls out. 'I know the perfect place near here.' I might even buy you a cupcake if you're good, she thinks, if my guilt over the wedding mixed with generosity of spirit holds out.

HUNGRY FOR LOVE

The answer appears to be yes, but the rest of the walk is conducted in silence.

The man at table three is lingering over his coffee. Dan, behind the till, clenching and unclenching his fists underneath the counter, just wishes he would leave. And he recalls how easy it had been the other day to stand up to those yobs kicking the homeless man, righting a wrong. Maybe in this case, it's the man at table three righting the wrong. For there can be no doubt, the meeting was as bad as could be expected and yet now this unwelcome financial cuckoo in loud braces is casually sipping a cappuccino—for free. Dan's people pleasing skills are nothing if not overdeveloped. If he's so keen to close down my cafe, thinks Dan, why be such a hypocrite as to swallow my profits. And in his mind, Dan spools an elaborate fantasy about shoving the man and his brash braces into the industrial sized Magimix and switching the speed to fast.

And then the cafe door opens and in walk two people, one of whom is Jax.

For the second time today, Jax breathes in the familiar toasted sugar aromas and feels the knots at her shoulders loosen. Sonya is putting the finishing touches to a new window display of various baking tins hung by wire. She gives Jax a little wave. Jax suspects the wave is female semaphore for Back Off, I Have Slept With Dan.

'It's bigger than it looks on the outside,' says Majella.

'Ooh, matron,' smiles Jax, heading towards a table and feeling strangely elated. She has spent the last ten minutes in her mother's company and they haven't rowed. Admittedly they haven't spoken, either, but she wants to look on the bright side.

Dan approaches their table, notepad in hand.

'Dan, this is my mother. Mother, Dan owns this fabulous Barracks Bakery.'

Dan winces, afraid that the man in braces might overhear this reflected pride and seek to puncture it.

Jax studies the specials blackboard and selects a new variety, a bagel-shaped banana sponge drizzled with lemon buttercream and chopped pecans for herself, and suggests the signature chocolate velvet cupcake for Majella. Dan writes down the order, but seems distracted. Everyone's mind this afternoon seems to be elsewhere.

Jax is sitting at an angle to Majella who is half-heartedly taking in the sights of the cafe, the poured concrete floor and chrome fittings. The other customers are Asian tourists studying maps, two teenage girls comparing iPhones, and a chap in braces lost in thought. No one is likely to come up and ask for Majella's autograph.

Jax cannot remember the last time she ate out with her own mother. Majella believes in telling you what to eat, not in providing what you might enjoy. Sitting opposite her mother Jax is reminded of those many meals with Jonty where the restaurant food was delicious but where they ate in complete silence. Where what she really hungered for was the naughtiness of Pablo, the fun of Brian or the culinary inspiration of Dan. And now here she is with Majella, wanting to believe that the frayed maternal cord is not about to unravel.

'I'm sorry I cancelled–'

'How was your little cookery–?'

HUNGRY FOR LOVE

They both speak at once, which Jax can't help thinking sums up their silently competitive relationship brilliantly. Jax defers to her elder. Majella face breaks into a syrupy smile.

'Your little cookery course. How was it?'

Jax purses her lips. I'm about to talk to my mother about food. I'd almost prefer to be berated for the wedding. She hesitates and wishes Dan would hurry up with the tea.

There are several ways of answering Majella's question and all would appear to be booby-trapped. Jax could say the course was awful, unhelpful, boring, a waste of time. No one could be a better teacher than you, Mama. Or she could rhapsodise about the sun-washed setting, Pablo's talent, and the meals which made her swoon with delight. She could shock her mother by describing the ego boost of sex with two ravenous men. And yet she says nothing. She has a sudden realization that in her mother's orbit she becomes like a child. Regression, Caryl's therapist calls it. Both daughters have the tendency, apparently. Jax is an adult sitting with her mother yet she feels cowed and inarticulate.

'It was fine.' This is as much as Jax can muster by way of reply.

Dan arrives with a tray bearing cakes and a pot for two. He sets it down on their table and proceeds to unload it.

'You should write an article about it,' says Majella, unaware that this was the general idea. 'For your little magazine.'

'Oh, but I hate working for *Your Day*,' blurts out Jax, surprising even herself. Winning her old job back suddenly doesn't seem so vital.

SOUR CHERRY TART

Dan drops the pastry forks. They clatter to the floor and he turns to replace them.

'Then it's a pity,' hisses Majella, half turning to check that Dan has in fact moved away, 'that you cancelled the wedding, because now you'll have to support yourself. For the rest of your life, I should imagine.'

How quickly it always comes to this. And Jax has to concentrate on all the tea paraphernalia to stem the childish tears which threaten to fall.

Dan reappears and sets fresh forks down on napkins. 'Ladies,' he whispers. Jax can feel the heft of him at her side.

He hesitates, hoping to eavesdrop further on Jax's career plans, fearful she might leave London if she stops writing for *Your Day*, but sadly no tables in the vicinity require clearing or wiping. Reluctantly he slopes back to the counter.

Jax grabs one of the new napkins and dabs an eye. She is a grown-up. She has been betrayed by Jonty and yet fought back. I do not have to stay crushed. She can almost taste the fortifying elixir of independent thought. Between her and her mother sits a plate of cakes. In another era they would be rapiers, or pistols on a velvet cushion.

Jax reaches for her weapon of choice. It's a speckled sponge moist with banana, the butter-cream zingy with citrus zest, and nibs of nuts for extra crunch. She knows where she is, with a cake this well conceived. She licks a fleck of buttercream from her lips and looks Majella straight in the eye. 'I had no choice but to cancel my wedding, Mother, because as I know Caryl has told you, Jonty cheated on me.'

161

HUNGRY FOR LOVE

'Oh, for God's sake, Jacqueline.' Majella smacks her cup down on its saucer; Dan winces. 'How could you have been so selfish as to ruin the day?'

All Jax's nerves go taut. 'Selfish?' This is the word Jax has been expecting all along. Not least because it's remarkable how often people accuse others of the attribute most applicable to them. 'Better that I put myself first, for once, surely, than that I ruin my life forever?'

Majella picks up her cup again, and sips her tea.

'But if you're worried about the money, Mother—'

Majella waves the comment away. 'The insurance covered all that.' She grimaces. 'But that week of all weeks. Had you no consideration? I had people ringing me all day.'

Jax frowns. 'People rang you?' Jax cannot imagine any of her side of the aisle ringing Majella to commiserate.

'The vicar. The bell-ringer.' There's a tinge of fury in her voice.

These were surely courtesy calls. 'Who else?' Jax says.

Majella can barely contain herself. 'The press. A guest must have leaked it and they were crawling all over me. Lawyers for my publisher had to work jolly hard to get them off the scent.'

Jax catches her breath. 'Your publishers did that for me?'

Majella stiffens. 'Not for *you*. For the book. It's vital we don't have any bad publicity in the run-up to the launch of *Food of Love*. Although at this rate—' She breaks off and glances around the room, but no one is listening. No one knows who she is. It's possible no one even cares. And for a second Majella glimpses the freedom which comes of anonymity. It is at once intoxicating and absolutely terrifying.

SOUR CHERRY TART

Jax hands grip the side of the table, blood draining from her knuckles. She has never had a row in the Barracks Bakery, in this precious space before, and it's making her feel sick. She has a fantasy of all the cakes in the cafe exploding, of buttercream splattering the bare brick walls, of Dan driving through in a tank. Yet one more reason to be annoyed with her mother. 'The book,' she seethes. 'It's always about the bloody book, with you, isn't it? My fiancé betrays me and you're worried about the impact on your book—' She spits out this last word.

But Majella is not paying attention. She's off on a riff of her own. 'So Jonty had an affair? You don't know how lucky you were. Such a catch. So polite. Always said how much he enjoyed my cooking. And it's not like you've got them queuing up, is it? Anyone would think you had other options. Men aren't like London buses you know. One day you'll wake up and realise that you're on the shelf, feeling no more attractive than a sagging bag of flour—'

Majella's face whitens and she stands up abruptly, pushing her stool back with her calf muscles. She walks towards the door and then turns abruptly. Jax braces herself for a final riposte—the success of her mother's books is intricately linked to the woman's mental equilibrium. But having approached the table, it is not Majella's tongue but her hand which appears, reaching out to grab the uneaten chocolate velvet cupcake, before Majella strides purposefully back towards the street and the noise.

A gust of air from the street ushers in the noxious odour of diesel fuel.

BITTER GOURD CURRY

'...and when you slice into them they create the most attractive little black pinwheels which add visual variety to the curry table. This is important because along with smell, it is our eyes which stimulate the appetite...'

From behind the carved oak, Dan watches Jax staring at her lap for several minutes, a camouflage napkin balled into her fist. Eventually, she puts the napkin on the table and spends a while flattening out its creases.

The man in braces approaches the counter. Dan is relieved to have it as a barrier between them. The man tries to pay for his coffee and Dan says he wouldn't hear of it, and so the man wins. As the man walks towards the door, Dan sees him give Jax a discreet nod as if buying livestock at auction. Dan's stomach falls away.

Jax gathers up her things and approaches the counter. 'Sorry about that. My mother had to leave—' she begins, but then stops.

Dan's eyes are not on her but on the door, now being tugged closed. He stares through the window of the door. The view beyond his cafe is a blur. The pavement outside is full of people on the move, but Dan doesn't want movement. He wants stillness or even retreat. He doesn't know what he thinks and he doesn't know how he feels.

Then he does feel something, something brushing against his hand, light and soft as a feather. He glances down and registers another hand on his, delicate yet lightly tanned, the nails pink and healthy. He looks up and finds himself tripping into Jax's eyes. For the first time he can properly see that they are hazel, with the faintest fleck of honey. He longs to say something to her, to unburden himself, but also knows that he doesn't want to break the spell of Jax holding his hand. Were she to withdraw it now, he would suffer an intense sense of loss.

'What?! They want to close you down?' Jax is trying to whisper but she is, Dan can tell, appalled. 'Are you sure?'

She and Dan have moved to the kitchen at the back; Sonya watched the two of them go with an expression close to mutinous. In their suspicious absence she twists the plastic bauble in her earlobe until the hole bleeds.

The kitchen is perfumed with warming spices, where yet more chocolate velvet cupcakes are rising good-temperedly in the oven. Jax feels she has been admitted to the inner sanctum of holiness and would love to luxuriate in the privilege. But Dan's obvious pain, his misery draining the freckles of their lustre, demands her attention. 'Dan?'

'That's how the world of finance works, apparently.'

'But that's bonkers. You're full all day. Every day.'

'Full, but evidently not profitable enough. There's only so much you can charge for flour and eggs.'

'Listen to you. We're not talking cakes here, Dan, we're talking works of art, of inspired imagination. Don't they realise? Have you told them?'

'That's what today's little chat was meant to be about. An opportunity for me to put my case. To make me feel like they're including me somewhere in this equation.'

'And?'

'Well, he ate one of my chorizo panini, so maybe all is not lost.' He attempts a smile, but it is clear that for once

HUNGRY FOR LOVE

Dan's faith in the transformative power of leavened batter is wavering.

'But this is ridiculous. Time spent in this cafe is therapeutic.'

He wants to hug her, for this deep connection they share about the importance of cake, this burnished way of seeing the world. Hug her, or even eat her, if only the connotations weren't so sleazy. Jax is too pure for that.

He starts pacing the kitchen. 'When I was in the army, we were often fighting political battles, about cuts in defence spending, the reduced amount of kit. So when I set up this place, the one thing I was determined to avoid was a crisis in funding.'

'Well, we'll just have to raise some money and keep it open.' He can tell she hasn't a clue how to do this. Maybe the sugar has gone to her head.

Dan shakes his head. 'They're not closing it down. They're knocking it down. Compulsory purchase order.'

'Bloody hell. Knocking it down?'

'They're developers and they want to build flats.'

'And make a financial killing. Sharks like Jonty, stuffed with testosterone.' She pauses. 'So what are we going to do?'

'Fuck knows.'

Jax has never heard Dan say anything so fruity. She also sees a persimmon flush enflame his cheeks which is quite ravishing. It's a moment as intimate as any of her recent sexual couplings. A vein in his neck has started throbbing. She bites her lip.

Dan is also surprised to have sworn. The adrenaline and banter of the barrack room is a lifetime ago. And yet his skin tingles. Despite his tremulous despair, there is something perversely glorious about having a conversation of this magnitude, of this import, with Jax. What are *we* going to do? she had asked. As though they're a couple and are discussing things of significance to them both, hushed and intimate things, that will affect them for the rest of their lives. Which is the moment he remembers that this matter of redevelopment is going to affect his life. Soon he will be unemployed, most likely unemployable—two careers down—and without ready access to the love of his life. The news, confirmed this afternoon, has felt like someone has taken a meat mallet and pulverised his very soul.

'I should never have left the army,' he mutters to himself. He feels diminished. And yet just standing with Jax makes him want to fight. He stops pacing. 'When the going got tough in Helmand and we routinely looked like we were beaten, we always used to say: rock bottom is a solid foundation to build on.'

'Good. So let's create some publicity. Let's start a petition. I'll mention it in *Your Day*. We keep a page for topical events. Usually quirky items like outfits for pets-as-bridesmaids. But this can be a new spin on things.'

'We don't have long. They're talking days.'

'Ah,' says Jax solemnly. 'That's no good then. But we can still do the petition online, like on Twitter.' And she reaches into her fashionably capacious bag for her phone, ready to draft something dynamic and flinty; the very opposite of cake.

'We're going to show those bastards in private equity just who they're dealing with. Grab me that pad of paper.'

HUNGRY FOR LOVE

Jax has never heard Dan sound so fierce, so assertive. But rather than finding this off-putting, a bit too Jonty-ish, it's as though Jax has bitten into one of Dan's exquisite Belgian Surprises, where the sponge contains a hidden spoonful of melted chocolate oozing seductively on to the tongue. She can sense a peculiar energy in the room, which thrums through her body and which makes the hairs on her arms stand on end. She likes it when men are men, it just that she likes it even better when they also treat women as equals.

'Sorry I barked just then,' he begins, rotating his shoulder, 'but the idea that someone wants to take this little place I've built up and smash it to pieces is beyond words.'

Suddenly, he spins and sniffs. She hopes to God he isn't starting to weep, but evidently the sound—alert, appreciative—is instead a practiced olfactory test as to the doneness of the chocolate velvets. Ever the baker, he expertly removes two large patty tins from the heat and taps the cake tops, smiling at the way they spring back obediently. They are his little soldiers, regiments of the tempting, ready for battle.

Although in that moment they look to Jax, without their traditional swirls of buttercream, exposed and scarily vulnerable.

Rocky Road

'…which makes it the favourite of school lunchboxes, teatimes and picnics. Different crushed biscuits can be used in the mixture, but most people prefer the traditional digestives and this is definitely one time when innovation is wasted…'

Brian is working at his laptop. Or rather he's seated in front of his laptop but staring out the window. Brian's flat faces east down the Thames. Its floor-to-ceiling windows face the Houses of Parliament and Big Ben, sights so familiar as to be not just invisible but ignorable. He is conscious of this sacrilege—tourists endure hours of jetlag just to see them—but it's a fact that what people remember from their trips abroad are not the tourist destinations, the landmarks, the beauty spots, but the incidentals: the sweary taxi driver, that overpriced bistro, the pigeon that craps on your head.

The personal is so affecting, thinks Brian. It's the engine of change. Which is why he has spent the morning googling the Barracks Bakery. Something about the place has got under his skin. Or more specifically, under his tongue. He can still feel the smoothness of Dan's frosting on his tongue this morning. He can visualize the rugged interior with its post-industrial furniture, together with the sumptuous displays of baked goods giving the bakery's clients a sense of being in safe hands—and Brian a glimpse of serenity. And that brownie! The grain of that angelic blonde brownie, damp with ground almonds and white chocolate, yet ethereal at the same time.

Brian's experience of eating Dan's food has been personal; it has conjured up for him a time when cake

169

was king, when Rosario the maid would bake him treats after school, for those empty hours before his mother would return from afternoon tea and after she went out for cocktails. No wonder he has a sweet tooth, and a tendency, as his doctor has observed, if he skips all those gyms, to pile on the pounds.

Some of Dan's confections appear as photos on the website. Brian thinks the site needs a revamp. But still, he can't remember feeling this fired up by a taste sensation since he was sent away to summer camp and tasted marshmallows toasted over a campfire. And there have been many taste sensations over the years. Which reminds him of Jax, when it shouldn't.

Sweet Jax, in bed, and the creaminess of her skin. One of his mother's most cutting assessments when she was alive was to have described Brian as having enthusiasms. Which was harsh, given her own marital history. But there is no denying that with properties on four continents—to relax in, when not in one of his gyms—Brian is a man of appetite. And so, perversely, the moment at which he knows he mustn't string Jax along is the moment that he knows he has fallen for her.

To push aside thoughts of Jax's arousing qualities, Brian returns to Google and scans the Barracks Bakery's web page. He opens up the menu page and salivates over the descriptions of the sausage popovers, the Key lime pie cupcakes and his favourite, the beetroot chocolate loaf. He reads another page, describing Dan's ethos for the bakery and warms to a man who can write about cakes as if describing close friends. The world seems to be peopled with those who have found their own inner source of contentment. Brian—global citizen and currently long on property—is aware that he envies that.

The doorbell rings. He folds down his laptop with a sigh and stares out at the Thames. The stranded passengers on board the duck boat are clearly no closer to being rescued.

Jax, as she leaves the bakery carrying an enormous bag of chocolate chip cookies, practically trips over Jonty. He is kneeling on the ground, as though tying shoelaces.

'Jesus, Jonty, stop stalking me.' She is about to become a national crime statistic, attacked by someone she knows.

'Jusht tying my shoelaces,' he reiterates, standing up. The slight woozy sway is the giveaway.

'Don't be daft, you're wearing slip-ons,' she says, more tolerant than she expected to be, of the lie. She wants to remember that once a liar always a liar, but the memory of his declaration of love in her bedroom last night is twitching on some internal thread still linking the two of them. 'Anyway, what are you doing here?'

'You're always in this bakery. You practically live in the place. Can we talk?'

'About what?'

'About us.'

He says ush, but even so, in spite of herself, she is hooked.

'What about Miranda?' She must protect herself from pain.

'What about Miranda?'

Pavement conversations with drunks—she knows this concretely from past experience with Jonty—rarely rise above this level of verbal dexterity. 'I'd've thought that was obvious.' She doesn't mean to sound spiteful, but he has thrown her by appearing out of the blue. Her emotions around him are clearly still volatile. And she's in a hurry, on her way to the hospital. A message from Nurse Alison has said that Caryl has come round from the sedation and asked specifically for her. She starts to walk in the direction of the hospital. 'There can be no "us" with Miranda around.'

'Miranda's sick.'

Jax stops. Maybe Miranda is dying. So maybe Jonty is only pursuing her on the rebound. She feels a muddle of sympathy and anger and turns, to find that Jonty has not moved. In fact he seems glued to the pavement. Or rather his feet appear to be; the top half of him is ever so slightly at an angle.

'Jonty, I need to get to the hospital. Walk with me.' She envisages Miranda and Caryl in adjoining beds and feels a lurch of anxiety.

Jonty doesn't move. Jax recognizes his controlling tendencies, and her own weariness of them. She turns away and sets off again in the direction of the hospital, through the royal icing maze of stuccoed Georgian houses. Each block has its own resident geriatric, out for a walk with various types of toy dog—chihuahuas, Scotties, dachshunds; rodents, in tubular tartan coats.

'So how's things, babe?'

His breath feels warm on her neck.

'Do you mean after my ex-fiancé lunged for me last night with a knife?'

'Oh c'mon Jax, I miss you.' Mish you.

'You're drunk. And you were telling me about Miranda. You said she was sick.'

ROCKY ROAD

She is confused by her own equivocation. Ending their relationship would have been easier if Jonty had ever raised his fist to her. A definitive moment, a crossing of the line. Although she knows that for some women not even violence provides sufficient stimulus to leave. For others it would have been one flirty text that did it. For others, the first affair. Or the ninth. Or the next round number. For others it would be the cross-dressing, the gambling debts, the black eye. For others there might never be a self-imposed boundary.

Jonty trots ahead of her, and speaks while walking backwards. 'Miranda's sick. All the time. Makes herself sick, after every meal.'

Yes, thinks Jax. I know all about Miranda's bulimia. I shouldn't know, but I do.

'I'd never noticed it before, but she didn't eat a thing in the Maldives. Awesome fish, bloody expensive, and she threw the lot up. I flew home early.'

'Perhaps she's pregnant.' Jax says this drily, but a chill sweeps through her in case this is true and the infidelity is then utterly beyond redemption.

'Pregnant?' Jonty pauses. You can almost see the cogs of his brain whirring. 'Nah, we used condoms. I did that for you, babe. I wore condoms for you.' And he reaches out to ruffle her hair.

Jax feels every cell in her body go cold. She steps back. 'Don't touch me.'

'Babe–'

'You did that *for me*?!'

'Yeah. She's one mega-fucked up babe, Miranda is.'

'You used condoms out of respect *for me*?' Jax takes another step back. 'When you were engaged to me and sleeping with another woman?'

HUNGRY FOR LOVE

Through the mist of whisky, Jonty is dimly aware of something, but he can't quite make sense of it. 'Yeah.'

Respect. Me. And Jax raises her arm, swings it in an arc, and brings the mighty sharpness of a stiff khaki bag containing dozens of cookies down to bear on Jonty's right temple. Caught off guard, he loses his footing and crumples into a mushy pile of newly excreted chihuahua poo.

KOEKSISTERS

'…and that's this South African sweet treat, where plaited and fried dough is firm and chewy and can be drizzled in syrup. They are the perfect cake to dip into coffee, but maybe not when they have been also coated in another popular variation, desiccated coconut…'

Jax reaches the hospital out of breath, the word condom still pounding in her head in time to her racing heart. At one point, waiting for the green light at a pedestrian crossing, she'd been shocked not to find steam leaking from every pore. She pulls out her mobile from the depths of her handbag to switch it off and sees that she has two missed calls. Both from Majella. No voicemail has been left. Jonty, she assumes, is still slumped on the pavement.

Nurse Alison escorts Jax into the Intensive Care Unit. Jax thinks that if she ever found herself in a room with such melancholy lighting and background monitor beeping she'd slit her wrists. No, not slit her wrists! That's the elephant in the room. She mustn't think of elephants.

Caryl is sitting propped up in bed. She reminds Jax of a militant child in a high chair, refusing to be fed. Her arms below the elbows remain under the bedclothes, so it's impossible for Jax to tell if the giveaway bandages are still in place. Still, there is no sign of the intravenous drip today, which Jax hopes is good news.

The staff are busy at their pieces of equipment, like altar boys tending to sacred vessels. As Jax is shown in, they melt away to offer some privacy. And as they do, Jax realises with mild alarm that she hasn't prepared what to say or how to be. Perhaps she should have brought grapes. But then again, under the circumstances, maybe not. Jax so longs to act with ease that she now feels acutely self-conscious. She decides to leave asking Caryl how she feels to Caryl's therapist.

Jax approaches the bed. On the bedside table she catches sight of Caryl's reading matter. It's a book of Tennyson's poems and Jax is reminded of Desmond. 'Come, my friends, 'tis not too late to seek a newer world'. She shudders. Presumably Caryl had meant to find a newer world in death. She leans in to kiss Caryl's cheek and slips an arm around bony shoulders. She must reek of sugar and ovens and eating, for which she wants to kick herself.

'I'm sorry,' whispers Caryl.

'That makes two of us,' laughs Jax, perching on the bed.

'Is mum here?' The shadow of Majella is ever-present and deep.

Jax shakes her head. 'She was, earlier. But we went for tea and had a row.'

'No change there, then.' Caryl leans back onto her pillows. 'Is she cross with me?'

'Majella's cross with everyone, don't you think? And very sniffy about my course.'

'Oh yes, how was it? Tell me everything.'

Jax thinks Caryl looks beleaguered. Which is hardly surprising: she's been on a journey to death and back. Perhaps Alison is right, that Caryl regrets surviving. She longs to ask Caryl why she did it, what led her to want to cut herself open. Madness, presumably, but with some essential logic underpinning it. Caryl—surgery doctor, BSc Hons, and MRCGP—would surely know.

'How was the course? Extraordinary.' And Jax spins a tale about the sun and the hotel and the three musketeers:

KOEKSISTERS

Conrad and Pablo and Brian. She finds the telling of it all rather difficult, having decided at the outset that she mustn't mention food. Naturally, she crashes several times into the hungry elephant in the room—sex with Brian she describes as 'delicious'—but by and large she manages to avoid mentioning either cuts or consumption.

'You slept with *two* men?!'

Jax sees a dab of colour grace Caryl's cheek. It's an encouraging sign, but one which also reinforces the overall pallor. But it might mean that Caryl wants to pull through. Jax redoubles her efforts, playing up to the tale. 'It's fair to say I've become an absolute slapper. And listen to this: one of them has even jumped on a plane and followed me here!'

'Oh my god, that's so brilliant. And so naughty. Good for you.'

'Not that anything's happening–'

'That I don't believe! What's that in your hand?'

Jax glances down. She'd forgotten about the magazines, freebie copies from work. Not *Your Day* but sister titles from the same publishing house. Although not the food ones, obviously. She digs into her handbag and lays the glossies on the bed.

'Not that bag, the one the colour of army tanks. The squashed one.'

Jax experiences a flash of panic. Cookies. In Caryl's room. She almost expects Nurse Alison to come storming in with sniffer dogs. Raise your hands in the air and put the illegal substances on the floor where I can see 'em.

'It's nothing. Just something from my friend Dan's place.'

'Ah yes, Dan from the army. The bakery you're always going on about.'

HUNGRY FOR LOVE

'I do not.' Jax has forgotten how annoyingly perceptive her sister can be.

'You practically live there,' says Caryl gently. She leans forward and touches the bag. The bandages at her wrist have been replaced by gauze dressing. Its gossamer delicacy hints at an even deeper fragility. 'But it's torn, Jax. Why are you carrying around a torn paper bag?'

To match your torn wrists, Jax wants to say. I want to take away your pain. 'I've just socked Jonty round the head with it.'

'What?!'

'Jonty's been drinking, has dumped Miranda for her bulimia and wants to get back together. So I clouted him with cookies.'

'Pity the bag wasn't filled with your Year Seven hot cross buns. Remember them?'

Jax certainly recalls Majella's chipped canine tooth, the palaver of finding a dentist open on a Good Friday. 'Watch it. I can even make mayonnaise now.'

'And is that with Conrad, Pablo, or Brian?'

'You're disgusting.' But inside Jax is close to swooning, to hear Caryl larking around. She doesn't want to get ahead of herself but it is wonderful to think her sister is still alive, if slightly faded.

'And Jonty? Do you want to get back together with him?' Having knocked at death's door, turned its very handle no less, Caryl—overworked GP and boundaried clinical professional—is skilfully keeping the focus away from herself.

Tears spring to Jax's eyes. You don't have to worry about me, you're the one who's been unwell. She studies the battered khaki bag. 'Don't worry. Him and me, it's completely and utterly over. The pile of shit has ended up in a pile of shit.'

KOEK SISTERS

Caryl grins. 'Vey apt. Well done.'

Jax inches further up the bed. 'The only bit I don't understand is why it took me so long to break the thread. I should have dumped him weeks ago when you first told me about Miranda.'

Caryl shrugs. 'It had to be your decision. Timing is all. You wouldn't take a cake out of the oven before it was cooked.'

'That sounds like the kind of thing mother would say.'

'Maybe, but only if our mother was remotely insightful and empathic. What I mean is, one can't make a decision until the time is right. You can tap up other people for wisdom, but only you can rescue yourself.'

Jax wonders whether this is a gentle warning, that good Samaritans will not be tolerated.

Caryl stifles a yawn. 'Do you mind going now? I'm really sorry. I get really tired.'

Jax slides off the bed. 'Shall I leave these magazines here?'

Caryl nods and closes her eyes. 'Where are you going now? Back to dishy Dan at the bakery?'

A vein at Jax's throat begins to throb again at the memory of Dan pacing the room like a tiger, and swearing. 'They're trying to close it down.'

'Who?'

'Scummy developers. I'm going to spend the afternoon trying to get some publicity to stop it happening.'

Nurse Alison pops her head round the door. 'Probably enough now.'

Jax nods. 'I'm just going.' She leans in and strokes Caryl's hair, the way she has often wished Majella had learned to do.

Caryl still has her eyes closed. 'When I was little I used to imagine what I'd do if I was rich. I wanted to knock down ugly buildings, and build parks and gardens. Places of peace. With swings and swans. Even now it upsets me that so much of London is built-up. If I had loads of money now, I'd give it to your friend to fight for his bakery.'

'Pity I've gone and dumped the richest person I know, then,' says Jax with a wry smile. She turns to leave the room.

'Can you leave the bag?'

'What bag?'

'You know what bag.'

'It's empty,' Jax lies. It's full of crumbs, is what she thinks. But what she really means is, it's full of food.

Caryl opens her eyes. 'I am allowed to eat, you know.'

'I know. Or rather, I wasn't sure—'

'It's what they want me to do. I don't have to avoid taboo substances, like alcoholics or druggies. I just need to change my behaviour. After all, I can't live if I don't eat.'

And you don't want to live if you do, thinks Jax. She has the firm impression that to leave the food here with Caryl would be to invite tragedy.

'How about I share one with you,' she says. And she returns to the bed and pulls out the cookies wrapped in greaseproof paper. They're already in pieces, and some of the crumbs escape into the holes of the crocheted bedclothes. She holds out a fragmented rhomboid for her sister to take. Caryl's fingers, she notices, are thin and mauve, the nails ridged and brittle.

'Are you sure you want this?' Jax can feel her heart pounding under her clothes.

Caryl holds it for a long time, staring at it. It's as if she's unsure as to whether it's the nucleus of a dangerous atom or the final piece of a jigsaw.

FRIDGE SUPPERS

'...when they can sometimes be known as midnight suppers, meaning coming home after a night out, starving hungry. The key is to have a fridge which is stocked with a few essentials such as butter, some spring onions, jars of mustard and mayonnaise, some smoked fish...'

Jax lets herself into her flat. A dusky evening glow filters through the trees of the garden square. Her gang of friendly pigeons has gathered in the area outside her front door, warbling softly and practising their dance routines. They remind Jax of star-struck wannabes, waiting for her at a stage door.

After dropping her bag on the sofa, she goes into the kitchen. Saucepans, rolling pins and all the rest of Brian's recent equipment purchases have now dried on the draining board, complacent in having lost their culinary virginity.

Jax spends time putting them away and tries to make a note of what she has acquired, in case she ever needs to use them again. It occurs to her that, with all this kit at her fingertips, she might soon have to invest in a cookery book. Although not that one. Good grief, no.

She takes a shower. Recent feasts have given Jax a gentle swell to her belly. In the bathroom mirror she studies her silhouette—she is comparing herself to Caryl's emaciated frame. She approves of her lately increased appetites. In her preoccupation over what to do about Jonty, she had for a brief time recently forgotten to eat.

And as she towels herself dry she thinks of Jonty, toppling over into dog poo, and is aware that the abundant vat of love she had for him has now dried up. Perhaps in time she could have forgiven him, even gone on to marry him out of some form of guilt or spinelessness. But by doing that she would have ended up feeling as broken as an egg dropped on to the floor.

Wearing a dressing gown, Jax returns to her kitchen. The cupboards are now stuffed with newly acquired kitchenware, and she experiences a small thrill at its tucked away potential. No more Cup-a-Soup for me. She has the tools to make anything she wants. She might debeard mussels, singe peppers, whisk a soufflé, flambé crêpes. Desmond was a big believer in tools, preferring the garden shed to anything more sociable. Maybe this is why he turned to painting and poetry, as ready reckoners for life. Caryl's the one who has inherited his interest in things literary, judging by the draft novel she once showed to Jax, with its prophetic theme of self-mutilation. But as Jax stares into the fridge, contemplating the leftovers from last night's seductive feast, she can almost taste the impulse to be similarly creative.

Hurriedly she pulls out asparagus, eggs, cream and chives. At the back of the fridge she finds an unopened packet of smoked salmon and a tub of cream cheese. As though Brian had shopped on impulse and only decided what he would cook once he got back to her flat. She thinks of Pablo and feels buoyed by memories of his impressionistic style, a dollop of this, a splash of that. And of Brian who, by cooking specifically for her, has in some way validated her existence. I like you therefore I cook for you.

She recalls what Jonty said, that she would always need a prop in life. What on earth does he know?

She flings wide the cupboard doors and reviews the pans, the tins, the bowls and the sieves. They look sturdy and purposeful, ready for action. In drawers she finds knives, spatulas, whisks and wooden spoons. She strokes them, her new friends, and feels their solidity, their power.

She closes her eyes. Pablo told her to imagine what you want to eat, and then break it down to build up the dish from scratch. She imagines the taste of salt on her tongue, the way cream tempers it, along with a fuzz of nutmeg. She wants a backdrop of smoothness, but with a certain, lingering bite. Pablo believed she could do it. She remembers him peeling figs, and then unpeeling her, his fingers stroking her skin. And who is she to argue with evidently the world's leading culinary gigolo?

Am eating omelette/creamed asparagus/smoked salmon combo, she texts Brian

You've been cooking?

Was cooking, now eating!! She adds a smiley emoticon to her text for emphasis.

You dominatrix! Text me the recipe.

Made it up! Will have to write it down.

You'll be writing a cookbook next. Brian's text is accompanied by a winking face. In less than thirty seconds, another envelope sign pops up on her phone. *So, tell me what it tastes like.*

She thinks back to her first forkful, the mature saltiness of the fish, the sour greenness of the asparagus tips, the naughty ripple of nutmeg. *Orgasmic!*

Sounds like my kinda food. Something about Brian, or food, or both, has brought out Jax's inner slut. After an adolescence memorizing Cosmo's sex tips on the school bus, it's a relief to be in an adult relationship which permits such healthy filth. *In what way?*

Just the right amount of lubrication.

Her landline rings and she scrambles across the sofa for it, touching herself lightly underneath her dressing gown.

'Yes,' she says, breathily. Proper telephone sex is very underrated. It would be a heavenly way to round off the evening. 'Yes?'

'Jacqueline,' barks the voice. 'I've been trying to get hold of you all afternoon.'

SWISS CHARD

'…which, with its long leaves, deep green and burgundy colours, and refreshingly bitter taste, makes it the perfect substitute for spinach—especially in a recipe when something with more edge is called for, such as this tasty fish pie…'

'Yes, I've been trying to get hold of you all afternoon to say that I thought the cake thing from that cafe place was simply marvellous.'

Jax's heckles are up immediately. Majella does not normally phone to offer compliments. Majella does not normally phone to chat. Majella does not normally phone.

'Are you there?'

'Yes, I'm here. It's quite late.'

'So you don't want to talk to your poor old mum.'

Jax sighs and puts aside her mobile, with a pang for the interrupted titillation. 'So, what would you like to talk about?' She tries to sound interested, or rather to not sound cheesed off.

'Well the cake, for one thing. Quite marvellous. Almost as good as one of my own creations,' and Majella laughs, in a double bluff way to suggest self-deprecation and thereby still invite approbation.

'It's their signature line. Chocolate velvet.'

'Well, it's a great name. So dark and complex.'

Yes, thinks Jax, I can see why you liked it. She glances down at her mobile which is on silent. The envelope icon has appeared again. She wills herself to ignore it. 'Are you at home?' says Jax, floundering for conversational gambits. In the background she hears Parkin bark, on his king-of-the-castle cue.

HUNGRY FOR LOVE

'Yes, and Parkin's here and we've had a little light supper, some calves brains on toast, sautéed with a splash of cream and sherry, nothing special, I had them left over from a recipe I've been playing around with, not that I wanted much, I had a dreary lunch, waste of time, and then of course the lovely cake with you,'—not with me, thinks Jax, you stormed off to eat alone—'so I was wondering if I could ask you a favour–'

A wave of heat washes over Jax. It's one thing to defend oneself against an enemy's known traits, and quite another to have to contend with new characteristics. Majella is famously self-sufficient. Her appearance once on a local radio version of *Desert Island Discs* revealed a guest confident of catching creatures in traps, of knowing which species of mushrooms to avoid, of knowing how to wring the necks of fowls.

'A favour.' Jax doesn't care that it's obvious she's stalling. But Dan's intellectual property must at all costs be protected. If Majella asks for the recipe, she plans to put the phone down. She feels five years old, and petulant. 'It's just chocolate.'

'What, the cake? No, there's a mellow maltiness to it, which I reckon is Ovaltine. With a pinch of chili powder for a secret kick. With probably extra egg whites to bring out the softness of the crumb. And cocoa powder, for a fuller chocolate flavour. And more butter than normal, to compensate for the drier structure from the cocoa–'

Jax listens astonished. Majella has tasted just one cupcake and nailed its recipe exactly. A while back, Dan had let her in on his devised secret on the understanding that the information would remain strictly and forever Off The Record.

SWISS CHARD

'It's a very special cake, that one,' adds Majella. 'Made with love, I reckon.'

Jax seethes silently. Majella's performance would be impressive if it weren't so irritating, this proof of her mother's talent. Which also begs the worrying question as to why Majella has rung, if not for the recipe.

Jax thinks about texting Brian and co-opting him into phoning her mobile, thereby providing an excuse to get her mother off the landline.

'So, what do you think? Is it possible?'

'I'm sorry, mother, could you say that again. The line went a bit funny.'

'That's because you live in a basement, Jacqueline. Mould on the walls, I shouldn't wonder. But that Barracks Bakery, do you think I could use it for the book launch for *Food of Love*? It would be the perfect setting. And you could cover it for your magazine.'

'I doubt it. The cafe's about to be closed down. Compulsorily purchased. You know, totally flattened.' Jax hopes by her tone to suggest she can hear the wrecking balls in noisy action even as she speaks.

'Well, could you just ask?'

Jax can hear her mother's measured breathing, can almost hear Parkin's too—fetid and smelling of jellied dog meat, or more likely calves brains sautéed in cream and sherry—mistress and hound, controlling their breath in anticipation. Who would have thought Majella—negligent mother and outspoken critic of Jax's decision to end her own engagement—would like Jax's help in soliciting Jax's beloved Barracks Bakery as a venue for the launch of Jax's bête noire, the *Food of Love*. Jax can still recall the hefty first edition, artfully dotted all over the house, with its photo on the front of glistening langoustine tails tucked into herb-flecked polenta. Whenever Jax reads anything resembling a prawn on a menu she can feel her throat constricting.

Of all relationships, she thinks, the maternal pull is assumed to be the strongest. Is it possible, she wonders, to achieve redemption for one's soul whilst at the same time practising spite? And before she has realised what she is doing, she has, very quietly—as though guided by the stealthy fronds of mould said to stroke the walls of central London basements—put the phone back in its cradle with a satisfying click.

CASSOULET

'…sausage and pork heaven. The cooking time is long, especially with the soaking of the haricot beans beforehand, but there is something soothing about a slower pace and for winter days this dish is the perfect source of calming activity with delicious results…'

Brian is working at his laptop. Or rather he is seated in front of his laptop but staring out of the window. This, he knows full well, is an alarmingly regular occurrence. He has a well-stocked to do list this morning, but instead he is dreaming of Jax. Last night's text flirtation with her was frustratingly short-lived, and it reminds him of the way she had slipped out of his bed to return to London when they were on the course.

It's a role that usually falls to him to play, the disappearing lover. He smiles ruefully. Perhaps the universe is warning him off. But he can't stop thinking about curling up in the faint warmth of the sheet on her side, and this makes him want to text her. He picks up his mobile. He has followed Jax to London—although business would have taken him to the city anyway—not simply out of lust, but because he believes he needs her.

When he was little, Brian dreamed of rescuing his mother. Each night she would swan out for cocktails in another new gown, a new pair of heels, to meet Brad or Chip or Ramón. And Brian would lie in bed, desperate for the phone in the hall to ring, imagining a distraught mother at the other end, pleading for his assistance. Or he fantasized about stalking the streets of New York, discovering which plush bar she was in and striding across the floor to punch

HUNGRY FOR LOVE

Brad or Chip or Ramón on the nose. And in his dreams his mother would cling to him in tears, grateful to be rescued, promising never to leave his side again.

Recalling Jax's ankles hooked in ecstasy around his neck, Brian is convinced Jax has entered his life for a reason. And at the same time he worries that this is wishful thinking.

He puts the mobile—unused, yet hot in his hands—back down on his desk.

'Hey Brian—got any gel?' yells a voice from the shower.

Brian takes one last look at his laptop screen, at the cloud of camouflage graphics swirling around, before easing himself up off the chair to head towards his bathroom.

Dan is in the Barracks Bakery kitchen, drying patty tins and trying not to punch something. It's after the early morning rush. The school run creates a particular spike in Dan's daily sales; driving imported four-by-fours obviously makes women ravenous.

Army life taught him to be diligent about cleaning, but today his heart is not in it. The fragrance of sugar is in every thread of fabric, every inch of the oven, every groove of the oak counter, and it's turning his stomach. When he caught the whiff of the bedtime drink they use in their signature line of cakes, his chest heaved. Who knows how long this cafe will be open for. His sadness has mutated into an aversion to baking.

He has handed over masterminding today's specials to Sonya, who is delighted. The way to a man's heart, she hopes. Batter-encrusted wooden spoon in hand, she wonders aloud whether Dan has ever thought about making cupcakes with white chocolate instead of cocoa. He knows she means well, despite such a dated suggestion, so he says he will think about it. But inside he wants to weep. It disturbs him that he has lost the passion for his first love—his joy, his comfort in times of stress, his place of safety—and he doesn't know how to get it back. An emptiness gnaws away at him.

Brian reads this morning's sprightly little text from Jax and his face tightens. She wants to meet and asks to know where he's staying. He stands up and carries a mug of coffee over to the floor-to-ceiling windows; from this impressive vantage one might imagine Brian owns most of London. Jax doesn't know it but Brian's flat is barely a quarter of a mile from hers, just across the river. If it weren't for a huge seventies concrete monstrosity in the way, he would be able to see her garden square, possibly even into her bedroom where they had such fun the other night. And he would very much like to meet up with her again, but knows it's for the best if they don't. He doesn't want to hurt her, which shows him how in love with her he is.

The sound of cheerful singing in the shower wafts along the corridor on a cloud of almond and jojoba.

Jax waits three hours not hearing from Brian and then sets off. She had really hoped to discuss her dilemma with him, especially as she doesn't really want to mention Majella's request to Dan himself just yet. Dan is too kind-hearted for his own good. He'd agree to hosting the *Food of Love* book launch in an instant, even if the bakery had burned down.

She is also not a little annoyed that Majella can write off Jax's life choices and yet still come grovelling for favours. And she cannot shake the niggling idea that Majella is simply clutching at straws. Majella is clearly desperate;

HUNGRY FOR LOVE

Food of Love, Jax knows from all the posters over town, is to be published imminently. Not only is the café probably too small for the numbers, or the egos—what the media world calls talent—Jax imagines have been invited, it is Jax's belief that the rugged ethos of the place is entirely out of keeping with the image Majella would want to convey.

Sorry not to reply. In meetings. Bad reception. Love Brian. Slowly Brian deletes this text, the seventh reworked version of his reply to Jax. Never lead a girl on, as Rosario would advise—wagging a finger—when he used to promise to tidy his bedroom if only she would let him stay up until his mother got back.

Caryl is out of bed, sitting in a chair, a blanket over her unshaved legs. The top of her hand is bruised from where the drip was once clipped. Cautiously she's reading one of the magazines Jax gave her. She hasn't bought a magazine since she was about nine years old—it came with free Disney stickers—and certainly never a glossy.

Today she flicks past dewy photos of models advertising handbags positioned to suggest upholstered vaginas. It is hard to avoid the subliminal messages. The life dangled like a carrot is startling—wristwatches the size of side-plates, raincoats worn commando—and highly sexualised. The middle section is devoted to articles about female circumcision or child soldiers, stories for readers who want global issues along with their free silvery clutch bag. The food section is relegated to the back of the magazine, four pages of Vietnamese dishes for time-pressed readers who plan to visit Asia, after they've found a boyfriend.

CASSOULET

Caryl looks up. 'Are you OK? I wasn't expecting you.'

The two sisters kiss on the cheek. Jax can smell the scent of recently used shampoo and feels relieved. Maybe normality is returning after the anarchy of the previous week.

'How's things?'

'I think Alison wants to talk to you. I'm being discharged this afternoon.'

'That's fantastic.'

'Alison thinks it best if I stay with someone for a while. Do you mind?'

And in that moment Jax realises that she can think of nothing more wonderful than to have her sister move in. Conrad turned to her during a demonstration on the course a few days ago—Pablo's hand was up a chicken's flabby arse—and said that single women must beware of sliding into a spinsterish existence. They lose their libidos, apparently, and lounge about in pyjamas all weekend. Conrad reads women's magazines avidly, claiming to be monitoring the photographic competition, threatening Mike from time to time with resignation. His claim may be true. But Conrad is also, as a result, well versed in female issues and uses such knowledge regularly to get girls into bed.

'Can I talk something through with you?'

Caryl nods. It wasn't really a question as such.

'Mum's asked to use the Barracks Bakery for the launch party for *Food of Love.*'

'They're bringing it out again?' Caryl tenses up.

How could you have missed the posters, thinks Jax. 'New and improved, with twenty recipes for the gluten intolerant.

HUNGRY FOR LOVE

Plus a forward by some Z-list celebrity recovering from an eating disorder–' The elephant has escaped before she can reign it back in. 'Sorry, I didn't mean–'

'Should've asked me. Saved themselves a fee!' She catches Jax's expression of mild alarm. 'So, have you asked the man with the biceps? What's his name?'

Jax colours. 'Dan?'

Caryl smiles.

'I can't ask him. I hate to think of him being used.'

'How would it be using him? Didn't you say it was being knocked down? Surely a party might help?'

Jax's stomach twists. And she is back round her childhood dining table, sweltering in her itchy Christmas jumper, in August. 'It's what our mother does. Everything's always about her. Remember how we had to pose for those ghastly magazine shoots when we were small?'

'I told a photographer I was adopted. He wasn't remotely interested.'

'So did I! How funny.'

Although they both know it isn't, not remotely.

'I think I just want to keep these two parts of my life separate,' says Jax carefully.

'Hey, do you remember this?' Caryl leans awkwardly over to the bedside table for her hardback. She holds out the photo she's been using as a bookmark.

Jax takes it and sees that it's a photo of a birthday party, she and Caryl seated at the table. In front of them squats not the much-requested hedgehog cake with spines made from shiny chocolate buttons, but a drab yeasted savarin. The two sisters have scowls on their faces. Time has tinted the picture tangerine. Jax smiles at the irony: after years of being steered away from ready meals, the girls are the colour of commercial fish fingers.

Jax hands the photo back to Caryl with a soreness in her chest. Jax sees that her sister is mushroom pale. 'Do you want me to go?'

Caryl shakes her head, but half closes her eyes. 'My therapist came earlier today.'

Damn! Jax would have loved to have met her. She has long been curious, and imagines a tepee-shaped woman in kelim slippers and red, unruly hair.

'She's read some of my novel. Said it explained a lot.'

Another title for her sister's book pops into Jax's head: *Cook Back in Anger*. Jax remembers reading the early chapters, finding them uncomfortably raw. It is clear to her that the mother figure is only very thinly veiled. She remembers long ago once asking Majella where her own mummy was. A tea towel had come flying across the room, along with an instruction to start drying. And in a moment of clarity she sees Majella's cooking, her mastery of the kitchen, as a defence against something wide and desolate and overwhelming.

'Apparently, it's all about setting your own narrative—' says Caryl.

Jax isn't at all sure what that sentence means. Whether Caryl is talking now about writing, or life in general.

'There was a time when you and I didn't have a choice, we were too young. We had to do everything Mum said. But now you have a choice. Do you want to help Mum over her launch party or not? That's what you're in control of.'

'That's the nub of it, is it?'

''Fraid so.'

HUNGRY FOR LOVE

As the younger sibling, Jax is practised at deferring to Caryl. And yet now, having severed ties so spectacularly with Jonty, she wonders whether a similar momentum is building now for some sort of turning point with her mother. Jax remembers the bleating sheep, or goats, from the hotel of Pablo's course, with their dinky bells and ingrained dependency. They have, unlike her, in their endearingly ovine way, little choice.

'Well, she's asked for my help, which is a bit of a first.'

'Then you have a choice. You help or you don't help. It's up to you. You're in control.'

As they hug goodbye, Jax glances at the hardback lying on the bed, a copy of Tennyson poetry. Desmond had given both daughters copies—tooled leather, with marbled end-pages—when they passed their respective English Literature O Levels. Jax has her copy somewhere, back at the flat. She must dig it out and reread some of the poems. Especially *Ulysses*. 'Tis not too late to seek a newer world'. She wonders if it's too sentimental to imagine her father speaking to her down the years through classical verse.

Jax darling, we need to talk. Brian stares at what he has typed and then slowly makes the cursor eat up the letters one by one.

Caryl remains in her chair for a long time after Jax leaves. In hospital, with no distractions—no patients, no shopping, no binging, no reflux—Caryl has had ample time to think. Emotions habitually suppressed have had nothing to stop them resurfacing. She thinks back to the cookie Jax brought, crumbs in the bedclothes, chocolate on the

196

fingers. And what Caryl knows now is that she wants to taste food, not vomit. I am deserving of the food I eat. I am deserving of nourishment.

The door opens.

'You're looking thin.'

'Hello mother.'

'They're obviously not feeding you in here.'

'You said that the first time you came.'

Majella and I communicate like people snapping wishbones, thinks Caryl. Briskly, and in the vain hope of a positive outcome.

'Well, I've brought you some cassoulet. Build you up in no time.'

At nine hundred and forty calories per serving, thinks Caryl, from habit.

From a distance, the beige sludge in the Tupperware box looks like something she might have once thrown up. And for the first time, this embarrasses her.

'I hear they're bringing out *Food of Love* again.'

'Yes. The party plans are a bit awry, but if it happens, I hope you'll come.'

'If I'm feeling up to it.'

'That's why you should eat something. Get your energy up.' The Tupperware is waved aloft.

'Why is food the answer for everything, for you?'

Majella issues an embarrassed laugh. 'Darling, I'm a feeder, it's what I do.'

'Yes,' whispers Caryl, gripping the arms of her chair. 'You have fed my warped view about myself.' Caryl can feel her inner Jungian One punching a silent high five.

HUNGRY FOR LOVE

Majella flinches, as though fat from a pan has spat at her skin. When a recipe fails, Majella can be relied on to work out how to fix it. She knows she ought to reach out to her dear daughter lying in bed but she simply doesn't know how to cross the scrubbed lino or, more importantly, whether it will make any difference. Caryl, she has long thought, is like a difficult recipe which doesn't work, despite repeated attempts.

The conversation crumbles at this point, and Majella scurries out of the unit, taking her Tupperware box—her rejected frankincense—away with her.

As she strides to the tube, she has buzzing around her head something Desmond once said to her, quoting some writer or other, that failure is the condiment that gives success its flavour. Desmond, she finds, has a habit of popping up unexpectedly, like a belch.

She passes a bus shelter displaying her image, her slogan, and she thinks of her books and their reviews and the programmes and the interviews and, in spite of them all, the sight of her fragile daughter, so out of reach. She drops the Tupperware box into the nearest bin. Perhaps she should have brought flowers instead. She wishes she knew.

PICCALILLI

'…as they did in Victorian times. Making your own chutneys means that not only can you vary the strength of the seasoning, but you can ring the changes with the vegetables used. Jars of this make beautiful decorations in your own kitchen and to give away as gifts…'

The publishing house occupies two floors of a Dickensian building in Soho. Inside, the staircase is wooden, unvarnished and sloping from the decades of hopeful writers delivering precious manuscripts by hand. The owners have kept the interior deliberately austere, to hint not so much at the hard graft required to write a book, but at the clearly more arduous activity required to encourage people to buy it.

Toby has kept Jax waiting for ten minutes whilst he psyches himself up to meet a relative of Majella's. The last twenty-four hours have been horrendous. Banqueting managers at London's most fashionable venues—livery halls, restaurants, former slaughterhouses—have laughed hysterically down the phone at his requests for a booking. And he can't face another conversation with Majella and her bloody dog barking in the background. Toby is sure the mutt has got the scent of him already and would kill him on sight should they ever meet. Having chatted it through over breakfast with his shrewd, forensic sister, he plans today to tell his boss Will that he's resigning.

When he was peering at Jax through the spyhole in his door, he saw that she was reading a hardback. Well, that's a start. He tidies his desk again, and positions the coffee table book of which he is most proud, *Gardening for Grandees*, to face Jax. He has borrowed a chair for Jax to sit on, his own being a large Pilates ball which he hopes isn't too naffly visible over the desktop.

He opens the door and invites Jax to come inside. She smiles as she enters, putting her book away in her oversized bag. The preference for something so cumbersome escapes most men, including Toby. Toby prefers the trimmer security blanket of books. From what he glimpses, Jax's looks to be an old copy, with the sketch of a bearded man on the front.

Jax enters a room so crammed with books it could be mistaken for a walk-in library. She inhales the smooth aroma of intelligence, and of the pleasure in acquiring knowledge. Framed dust jackets hang like portraits of admired ancestors. There are even books lined up above the lintel. The offices of *Your Day* are decorated in a similar, mildly self-congratulatory fashion, but as Mike often says: 'seen one bride, seen 'em all'.

Jax comes straight to the point about the Barracks Bakery. Urgent assignments for *Your Day* have helped Jax adopt a crisp method for getting interviewees to open up in just the way she wants.

'You're suggesting a tiny cafe for one of the must-see events of the publishing calendar?' Toby is bemused. 'Don't you think it's a bit homespun? Your mother, after all, is a l-legend.' He was, he panics, about to say liability.

'It's not tiny, it's much bigger inside than you'd think. And it's quite funky in its own way.' And she pulls up its web page on her tablet, to show him the interior. 'Plus, it's not like you have many other options.' She hates herself for borrowing from Majella here, but in this kind of situation, it's a great line.

PICCALILLI

Toby can see that on some level, this young woman before him is most definitely Majella's offspring. The directness is undoubtedly her. But she has kinder eyes, a gentler smile, and the chestnut shade of her wild hair is authentic. It catches the sunlight through the Victorian paned window so that it appears almost haloed. He feels a welling in his throat.

'I'm going to resign today.'

'What?'

'I'm resigning. Whether at this cafe or not, your mother's launch will have to take place without me.'

'That's a bit dramatic, isn't it? We're talking a party in London, not on the moon.'

With a curt nod Toby concedes Jax's point.

'And anyway, won't you have to work a period of notice? The party's tomorrow. Although, at the moment, of course, you don't actually have a party. It needs organizing and you don't have a venue. You can hardly jump ship before then.'

'I'll take it as holiday–, as unpaid leave–'

This desperation. Toby turns to scrutinize his computer and Jax can tell that he's trying to hold it all together. Majella, Jax realises, has got to him, too. As her voracious appetite eventually gets to everyone.

'My mother's a difficult woman–' begins Jax, before stopping. She hasn't a clue what she is going to say next. 'Actually, I'm not sure I've ever really known my mother. But then,' she adds, 'I'm not sure we ever know our parents.'

Toby nods. 'My father died before I was born,' he says. 'Soldier. Northern Ireland. Boring old car crash, sadly. Still a hero to me, though. Wish I'd known him. Wish I knew more about him. One of the few things my mother used to tell me

201

was that he loved eating cockles and whelks. When he was on leave they'd go down to Brighton pier, buy little punnetts, dig out the flesh with tiny wooden harpoons. I've tried to like them–' Toby takes a deep breath. 'I've tried to like them, for him really, but they're revolting.' He attempts a laugh. Jax can see his eyes filmy with moisture. 'All chewy and vinegary.'

'I think they look like bogies.'

'Yes!' laughs Toby, relieved to meet a kindred spirit. 'Can't believe I've spent my life forcing univalves down my throat.'

'Well, that's easy. You wanted to get close to your Dad.'

'And? Are you here to get closer to your mother?'

'Touché.' Jax pauses. I've thought, she wants to add, of resigning as well, from *Your Day*. But Jax is not used to being the candid one in interviews, so she changes tack. 'But I want to help the Barracks Bakery too.'

'What do you mean?'

'It's threatened with demolition. Compulsory purchase. I wanted to start a petition, but we don't have the time. Mum's party would have been a great way to get it some publicity.'

'How far down the road are they with the compulsory purchase? My sister's a property lawyer. I could ask her to look into it, if you like?'

'I thought you were resigning. Didn't want anything to do with this party.'

Taking care not to roll around too obviously on the Pilates ball, Toby asks for her tablet and scrolls through the pages of the Barracks Bakery website. He reads about Dan's army career and feels a fond glow spread from his chest, remembering his own father. 'And you've spoken to the owners?'

PICCALILLI

'Owner. His name's Dan. We're both keen to know what you think. I'll help cook for the party. Just cupcakes and little bites.'

'And the publicity?'

'That's why I'm here. I can deliver the venue, which I imagine is no mean achievement at such short notice? You just need to pull out all the stops on the publicity front. Deal?'

Toby nods. 'And we won't even have to fork out for expensive caterers?'

'Like I say, it'll just be me and Dan and the bakery staff, so we'll invoice you accordingly.'

'You cook?' asks Toby, casually.

Men, even those like Toby who are a dab hand in the kitchen, love to hear that a woman cooks. It stirs in them hunter-gatherer memories of dragging the mammoth back to the cave.

It's a straightforward question, and one which normally Jax would try to avoid.

'Can I cook?' Jax is savouring the moment, as she might savour the bosky aroma of the first truffles in season. Truffles, or the melt of buttercream and moist sponge on the tongue in the perfect cupcake.

'Yes,' she says, simply, her heart swelling with pride. 'Yes, I can cook.'

SOUFFLÉ

*'...or savoury. The cooking mould is round or cylindrical, so that
the mixture can rise evenly. Cooking a soufflé is not as hard as it
sounds, but timing is crucial. It is worth noting that Cold soufflés
are really iced desserts which only look like cooked soufflés...'*

Dan is striving to achieve an authoritative air. As he places a
camouflage apron over Jax's head he thinks, randomly, of his
old parish priest—the one who buried Dan's father—laying
his hands on the bowed crowns of kneeling parishioners,
their hair enamelled by the light of the stained glass. He's
still not convinced that Jax's plan to hold a party for media
types in the Barracks Bakery will prevent its destruction—
his mother Caroline has joked that it might cause it—but
he knows that the presence this evening of Jax in his kitchen
is reviving.

He adjusts his own apron securely at the back of his
waist. He longs to rise to the imminent challenge; as if the
original decision to leave the security of the army and open
a cafe from scratch is not already an impressive accomplish-
ment.

He sneaks a look at Jax twisting her hair into a scrunchie
and almost pinches himself. Last night he finished another
of the thrillers to which he is partial, this one by a
Scandinavian. All the loose ends, tied up; with just a minor
one left hanging, seemingly inconsequentially, in case one
day the writer fancies another lucrative shot at the same
characters. Unlike in fiction, the universe is complex and
hard to fathom. Dan doesn't want to examine too closely
the sequence of events which has led his beloved Jax to ask to

SOUFFLÉ

work his stove, but he is beginning to trust in the universe. That it's mysterious movements might be empowering.

Dan and Jax are resolute that the menu must parade the kitchen at its culinary best: miniature madeleines in *zeitgeist* flavours of marmalade or pistachio, savoury tartlets in feathery filo pastry, and cascades of signature chocolate velvet cupcakes. Sonya is currently greasing tins and laying out paper cake cases. Caryl is sitting in the cafe proper, a long-sleeved top covering up the gauzy smudges at her wrists. She is folding khaki paper napkins into triangles.

Toby was in earlier, working with engineers on a discreet sound system. According to Toby—resignation letter typed, but as yet undelivered—everyone who had accepted the original invitation has confirmed for the revised venue. Diary columnists are being flexible. There has even been a febrile buzz on Twitter and the bigger foodie blogs, suggesting that the switch to the bakery is a deliberate marketing ploy, to emphasize the need for spontaneity in cooking. First, catch your hare, as Hannah Glasse is supposed to have advised back in the eighteenth century.

Dan is checking the ingredients, the resulting plunder from a frantic dash this afternoon around the cash-and-carry. Jax comes to stand next to him. He feels the warmth from her brush his skin.

'Private Jax, reporting for duty, Sah!' she salutes.

He grins. 'This'll only work if you're the same rank as me, from the very beginning.' His arms tingle so much it's as though his freckles are dancing.

For the next hour, Dan tells Jax everything he knows about baking cakes. He shows her how to tie the special aluminium fabric around his tins to keep the sides cooler which therefore slows down the baking to produce an even rise; how the cupcake cases need to be lined with a circle of parchment because chocolate batters are notorious for sticking; and how baking is a science, a precise equation between wet and dry, substance and air.

He takes a bowl and pours in a silky stream of sugar. Soft cubes of butter plop into the heap before he runs the mixer until the two are blended into a smooth, yet gritty, paste. After getting Jax to whisk eggs, he invites her to tip the mixture in, one third at a time, with a leisurely burst of speed from the mixer to combine the two before a longer burst to strengthen the cake's molecular structure. With each dollop of egg, Jax marvels at the way the batter relaxes as if breaking into a smile.

'Now for the flour. Flour not only stops the batter at this stage curdling, it also gives the cake its structure. It holds it all together.'

'A bit like you in the kitchen,' she smiles.

Yes, I'm the flour, Dan thinks. A bit dry and dull.

But in that moment, Jax is imagining stretching out her fingertips to stroke Dan's skin, can almost feel it as cool and soft as self-raising, the texture comforting and reliable. Lucky Sonya, she thinks, before snapping her attention back to Dan's masterclass in making cakes.

During the evening, Jax is aware that Dan's quiet authority in the kitchen has made her feel grounded. His codes and principles feel to her as though they must carry echoes of the deep wisdom of the ancients. The utensils feel solid and secure in her hands, as though she's been cooking all her life. She feels the heat from the oven as she slides in her first batch.

SOUFFLÉ

And as she beats more batter, aerates its structure, watches it slacken and turn pale, immerses herself in the textured alchemy of it all, she can almost believe that cake is redemptive. Sneaking a lick from the mixing bowl, the mixture tastes soothing, like an unexpected compliment. After the first few trays she can tell by the aromas when the cupcakes might be done. And as the smells of rising batter envelop her, she starts to feel all the fragments inside her melting into something golden and springy and whole.

'What on earth have I taken on?' she asks Caryl, during a rare window when the cupcakes are in the ovens and the equipment is being sluiced in the dishwasher.

'But you're loving it. I can tell.'

And Jax grins, because in truth she is.

Caryl's khaki origami is now stacked neatly into boxes. Jax takes one and wipes the sweat from her forehead. The air is cooler in the cafe than in the kitchen, but Caryl is still fanning herself with a piece of card.

'What's that?' asks Jax, holding out her hand. Perhaps Caryl has an admirer. Siblings need to know these things, if only to make the minute adjustments necessary to welcome in the new pulse which accompanies desirable happiness.

One glance and Jax can see that not only is it a business card but that it belongs to someone called Brian. His full name—with initials—telephone number and multiple addresses are embossed on both sides, in four languages, including Japanese. She grabs her mobile, scrolls for Brian's number and checks it against the printed hieroglyphics. 'Where did you get this?'

'He came in a couple of hours ago. Who is he?'

HUNGRY FOR LOVE

'Why didn't you tell me?'

'I wasn't aware I was meant to.'

'You think he came to find me?'

'He didn't mention you. I doubt he knew you were here.'

'So why was he here?'

'He came to see Dan. I explained everyone was busy tonight and he said he'd call another time. Most polite. American, at a guess. But I ask again, who is he?'

'Did you invite him to the party tomorrow?'

'No, I bloody well didn't.' Even siblings who have recently stroked death's sunken cheeks are allowed to get tetchy. 'How was I to know he's important? Is he important?'

Jax has stood up, grabbed her roomy handbag and is now tossing everything it accommodates onto the table. The very last thing to emerge, apart from an emergency tampon, is her pocket *A-Z*. She opens it at the list of streets and splays the spine. She checks the business card again.

'What are you doing?'

'What does it look like?'

'Throwing your toys out of the pram?'

Jax finds the page she needs and works out the coordinates. Then she starts removing her apron. 'We need to go. I need to speak to Brian. Find out why he's been ignoring my texts.'

'You can't go now. It's past ten o'clock. And you can't leave Dan to clear all this lot up on his own.'

Dan appears in the doorway, holding basins of freshly blended buttercream. He has only caught the very tail end of the conversation. 'You girls go. I reckon we're more than halfway through. And I can clear up here in no time. And then we can all be fresh for tomorrow night.'

SOUFFLÉ

Jax doesn't wait to be told twice. She attempts to pile her belongings back into her bag but mentally she's already in the car, across the river, and knocking on Brian's door.

It's some time after she and Caryl have left that Dan emerges from his now spotless kitchen. The cakes are nestling in their plastic airtight tubs, the buttercream is stored in the fridge. He has removed his apron, folding it carefully before putting it in the linen bag for washing along with all the tea towels. He is alone now, master of all he surveys. He begins the process of checking all the electrics, taking plugs out of sockets, lifting stools on to tables and switching off all the lights, and wonders what it will feel like when he eventually has to do this—very soon, he supposes—for the very last time. Maybe Majella's launch party will also be a wake, a final hurrah for the Barracks Bakery.

As he crosses the floor he comes to the table where Jax had been sitting with Caryl before she dashed off. She had seemed, so her thought, preoccupied. By the table leg he finds an old copy of Tennyson's poems. He picks it up. Maybe a customer left it behind earlier in the day. He will keep it on the shelf under the till until they come back for it, always assuming they remember where they left it.

Dan isn't much one for poetry—there was a brief craze for World War I poets on the base before the Sergeant at Arms had the copies confiscated—but idly he opens the front cover and reads the inscription: *to my beloved Jacqueline, I am proud of all your achievements, but more than that, I am proud of you, love Dad xx.*

Dan thinks this is the loveliest thing he has ever read. Raising the book to his lips, he kisses the inscription, inhaling the woodiness of the paper, with its cellular traces of paternal care. It is then that he sees something sticking out between the pages. Carefully he prises them apart, where a feather marks a poem. He read once that stray feathers are meant to be a sign that help is at hand.

He whispers the poem to himself, concentrating so as not to miss any of it. Certain lines reach out to him with their elegant poetic fingers, 'How dull it is to pause, to make an end, to rust unburnished, not to shine in use', and 'Tho' much is taken, much abides'. The whispered words fill his mouth like sponge-cake warm from the oven. And as he reaches the end, they loom up and touch his soul: 'To strive, to seek, to find, and not to yield'.

HUMBLE PIE

'…or the name given to a basic dish without pretension. Ideas as to what is a humble ingredient have changed over the decades, such as chicken which was once only affordable on special occasions such as Christmas and Easter. This modern version is made from pasta, tomatoes, onions and bacon and topped with cheese: humble, filling, yet delicious.'

She lies very still, not wanting to wake Caryl. Caryl, with her bandaged wrists and hospital printouts of healthy eating and tips for self-esteem. Self-esteem is a possession hard won. When Jax finally cancelled her wedding, it seemed that she had made a wise decision. But she sees now that it had been made without proper understanding. She had had to jettison Jonty not just because of what he had done but because of what she had allowed him to do. Walk all over her, treat her like plankton. And she allowed herself to be used in this way because she had felt so pathetically grateful. For all her quiet achievements, she has lacked self-worth.

She checks her watch and sees that it is still barely five o'clock. She should have listened to Caryl: 'According to Nurse Alison, I need to live a life of greater balance, give and take.' It was a hint that chasing after a man rarely ends well. She thinks back to last night and covers her face with her hands.

'Jesus, Jax. Slow down!'

All the green lights have been in her favour, which Jax takes to be a sign. But they are now on their third circuit of the Vauxhall gyratory, tangled up in the bus lanes and red lines, failing to find somewhere to park. On the other side of six lanes of traffic flirts a phallic block of upscale riverside apartments.

'Are you sure you want to do this?' asks Caryl.

Jax isn't sure what possesses her but she feels consumed. Brian's appearance in the bakery is like a worm at the end of a fishing rod.

'Look,' barks Caryl. 'Stop on that kerb there, by that dodgy-looking Eritrean caff. I'll keep the hazard lights on. And give me the keys.' Caryl holds out a bony hand.

'You can't drive.'

'I know. But also I can't not help you. Go. GO!'

Brian's flat is at the end of the corridor. Jax stands for a moment in the carpeted silence. Why on earth is she here, and what is she hoping to achieve? But she's unable to give herself an answer. The more she stands in the corridor, listening to the faint sounds of random domestic night-time routines filtered through the doors, the more she fears that if she doesn't act she will lose the chance to reach for something she has always wanted—whatever that might turn out to be.

She knocks, far too lightly at first; a television is on. She knocks more firmly, and hears the familiar jingle and bongs of the nightly news before they are muted. In some perverse form of muscle memory, her heart is beating as rapidly as when she first met Brian, out jogging.

When the door is finally opened wide, Jax is briefly distracted by the sight of the dark, yet glittering, river spread out before her, Big Ben and the Houses of Parliament brushed with a honey glow from the clever uplighting, and

HUMBLE PIE

to the right the London Eye, in cheeky pink. The sight is magical for being so vivid and so flawless, as in the ending of a movie—perhaps another blessed sign. She takes a step towards it, as if to touch it, to benefit from its civic perfection.

And then movement by the door catches her eye. Two shapes are now standing by the door, one in a white towelling robe. For some strange reason she notices that the robe has a hood. The French Lieutenant's Woman has come to call.

'Jax,' says the man in the hood, smiling broadly. 'What are you doing here?'

Already Jax is backing out of the flat, away from the view, away from what she thought she was reaching for, from what she thought she knew. And you, Pablo, she thinks, as she dashes back down the corridor towards the lifts. What on earth are you doing in Brian's flat?

'Jax,' yells Brian, pushing past Pablo. He has wanted to see Jax so badly today, it has taken him several seconds to compute that she is actually here, standing on the threshold of his flat. It's as if he has conjured her up purely out of his own strength of will; a sign, surely, that he is right to regard her arrival in his life as auspicious. 'Jax, wait,' he yells. 'Jax!'

But time wasted—telling Pablo to grab the keys, the numerous fire doors contriving to cut off his declarations to Jax, his slower progress than her in slippered feet—means that by the time he reaches the lift, she has gone. He thumps the wall and then has to lean against it, massaging his chest, gasping for breath. His global efforts to bully his core muscles into compliance, cannot completely keep back the simple passage of time.

HUNGRY FOR LOVE

Ten floors below him, Jax stumbles out of the lobby, shocked to feel the night breeze slapping at the wetness on her cheeks.

'I know a place,' says Caryl, grinding the gears.

The two sisters are leaning against a thick wall, looking out over the gently choppy Thames at Lambeth Palace. They are in Black Rod's Gardens, a small rectangular park with historical links in its name to protection and security. Side by side they don't look much like sisters, but Jax is surprised to feel that somehow they fit. Caryl hugs Jax from the side. It's like being hugged by a spindly tree. But a tree is still a tree when you're longing for shade, as *Your Day*'s agony aunt has been known to advise.

'I come here sometimes when I want a bit of strength.'

Jax tilts her chin at the bishop's home. 'Are you saying you've become religious?'

'Not exactly. But it's stood the test of time, that building, its faith. I take comfort from that, more than anything liturgical.' She gives her sister another sideways squeeze. 'I wish I could give you strength.'

Jax is unsure whether she merits such sisterly compassion. She might have earned it after Jonty and Miranda, but after sleeping with two such apparently international lotharios? She thinks back to Conrad by the pool, implying she could do better. Maybe Conrad has someone in mind.

'I feel such an idiot.'

'For sleeping with two men?'

'For finally plucking up the courage to run after one of two men, who now appears to be in a relationship with the other one.'

214

HUMBLE PIE

'That's ridiculous. Just because they're currently occupying the same flat doesn't make them a romantic item.'

'True. You're right. And anyway, I have a horrid feeling that's not what I was running away from.' For what she sees now is that once the door had opened wider and Pablo had appeared, she had been forced to confront the fact that she'd slept with both of them on consecutive nights! The heat of embarrassment washes over her. What perhaps started out as a cleansing holiday fling—fun, but not something *Your Day*'s agony aunt would advise should be taken seriously— had acquired, even if only in retrospect, a pleasing solidity. If it's true that after Jonty there are plenty more fish in the sea, then Pablo and Brian had been some of the tastiest to swim by.

But I've survived Jonty's infidelity, she thinks, and I shall survive this. After all, despite overfishing and global warming, the oceans are known to be reliably well stocked.

What she needs is a relationship with more equality, more balance, more give and take. Nurse Alison would approve.

'Look, why don't you invite Brian and whatshisname–'

'Pablo.'

'Brian and Pablo to the party tomorrow night,' says Caryl.

'No way.'

'Why not? It'll give Brian a chance to explain.'

'Because Brian's a man. And men let you down. They're like milk that's gone off. From now on, I'm going to starve myself of men.'

'Trust me. Starving yourself is never a good idea.'

HUNGRY FOR LOVE

Chastened, Jax stretches out an arm and grasps the rough stone of the wall. It feels firm and uncompromising beneath her hands. It has what Tennyson would call integrity.

'And anyway, it's no use crying over spilt milk.'

'Ha ha,' says Jax, cheerlessly. 'So what would you do?'

'I'd milk a different cow!' laughs Caryl, rather pleased with the dairy riff.

Jax glances at her watch. 'We ought to head back. Busy day of baking ahead tomorrow.'

'So, will you call Brian?' says Caryl, reaching for her BlackBerry.

'Maybe. But not now. Let's get the party out the way and then I'll call him.'

'You have time. Leave a message now,' says Caryl, holding out her BlackBerry.

Jax shakes her head. Just before she had pinballed her way back down the airless corridor she had advised both Brian and Pablo, in supremely colourful language, to do to each other what not days earlier each, in their own delicious way, had been doing to her. They will not, she suspects, be hoping to hear from her again.

For a long time, Caryl and Jax stand leaning over the wall, lichen rubbing off on to their clothes, as the sky deepens from mauve to midnight blue. At one point, a police motor-boat glides silently up river. And Jax sees that both she and Caryl are trying to do the right thing. A universal dream. 'I wish Mum was here.' And she squeezes her sister.

'God, we're a pair,' says Caryl, wiping her eyes.

PARTY FOOD

'...but of course if you serve caviar and champagne but your guests are bored, your party will fall flat. Keep your own stress to a minimum by serving food made in advance (and reheated if necessary) or having simple platters of tasty food for people to snack on. Enticing presentation is as important as what you serve...'

Where on earth is Dan?

Jax squeezes through the crush of people avidly licking their fingers. Sonya, and some of Sonya's friends have been doing a great job squiring trays of food around the room, holding them aloft when necessary, away from the talons of those greedy guests who hover with entitlement near the kitchen door of every party.

The Barracks Bakery is crammed full. Outside, for a distinctive entrance, Toby—a creased resignation letter burning a hole in his jacket pocket—has sourced a camouflage 'red' carpet which runs from the kerb to the cafe. Since technically it rests on council property, he has asked an office junior, one of the eager office interns—forsaking the five figure sum he could be earning in the City for a life of probable poverty yet artistic redemption—to keep an eye open for municipal killjoys.

As she presses past people, Jax can tell everyone at tonight's party is raving about the food, comparing favourite meals or swapping recipes. One, a statuesque beauty who models for a high street chain, is agreeing to be quoted by a short journalist—who can't believe his luck and wishes his mates down Walthamstow dogs could see him now—as declaring that cupcakes are better than sex.

HUNGRY FOR LOVE

Jax grabs one of the stools and uses it to climb gingerly on to a table, the better to peer over the heads of the hundred or so people squished into the room, the better to spot Dan. Of course, most of the people present are here for Majella and *Food of Love*, but one or two she has overheard only decided to come once the venue was changed, specifically to visit the Barracks Bakery. Or rather to indulge—under the guise of work—in its signature chocolate velvet cupcake. A woman she recognises from the oval desk of daytime news is eulogising over one as if it was a breaking news scoop. If only Dan were here to hear it.

The cafe is strewn with pea lights which make the bare brick walls appear to dance. Repeatedly they also light up in the silvery flashes from Conrad's cameras, as yet another guest arrives. There are the celebrities, eating more than their publicists advise; the journalists who might interview Majella; and the book critics whose job it is to assess where the revised imprint of *Food of Love* sits in the food-writing canon. TV researchers are thinking on their chunkily-shod feet about commissioning angles, and diets. There are the friends of Majella, intending to make up in consumption for the recently cancelled nuptial hospitality. And there is Mike, just disappearing outside again to have a ciggie in the street.

Everyone, she can tell—apart from Mike, of course, whose oral gratification is being met in other narcotic ways—is worshipping the food. Even Caryl is eating. From her lofty vantage point, Jax has just watched her sister reach out and take a normal bite out of an aubergine pesto tartlet. Caryl is talking to Toby. Jax hopes they're discussing literature. And then, remembering Caryl's manuscript, hopes they aren't. And then seeing their shy smiles, hopes they are.

PARTY FOOD

But she cannot see Dan.

She checks her watch. According to Toby's clockwork schedule, Majella is about to give a live TV interview to one of the nation's evening news programmes. Jax is desperate for Dan to be present, so that a sound bite about the Barracks Bakery's imminent closure can be worked into the discussion. Jax can easily see Majella. She's the one dressed in crushed raspberry satin, with boning under the chicken breasts to accentuate their creamy radiance. A tight crowd envelops her. A journalist pressed for time would liken them to bees round a honeypot, but Jax is reminded instead of a cow being milked. They will pump the sleekly bovine Majella for what they want, a quote, a glance, a waspish bit of backchat, and then they will scurry away to meet their deadlines.

Another of Conrad's flashbulbs illuminates the room, and for a second, everyone freezes and looks grasping and two-dimensional. She feels very protective of Majella in this moment, seeing her surrounded yet so apparently alone. The tiny hairs at the nape of Majella's neck appear luminous in the cafe's spun-sugar light. Jax's spine softens and the worry lines on her forehead slacken. And she has a sense of her mother as someone she might reach out to.

A final scan around the room and Jax sees Toby check the time. As he and Caryl make their way through the throng towards the door, Jax watches Toby remove his jacket to place around her sister's narrow shoulders. A warm feeling blooms across Jax's chest.

She steps off the chair and falls in behind Toby, now escorting Majella outside. They are met by the blinding glare of arc lights and the toots of passing taxi drivers. An

HUNGRY FOR LOVE

interviewer with the alarmed hair of a boy band is twiddling with his plastic earpiece, waiting for the cue from the distant production gallery. A chap holding a sound boom and a girl in jeggings are stood behind a cameraman. Jax doesn't know how long she has before the interview starts but with still no sight of Dan, she hurries to compose a one-liner just in case.

The chap with vertical hair takes his place in front of the camera and the crowd around him settles. A respectful silence descends, typical amongst people observing a stranger braving the void of a camera lens—the brain surgery is about to start.

Jax is handily standing next to Majella. She touches her mother lightly on the shoulder. 'Good luck, Mum.' She half expects the woman to dismiss the offer as unnecessary, but instead Majella turns her head and plants a tiny kiss on Jax's cheek. Jax works hard to resist the suspicion that such affection is all for the camera. Her mother smells wonderfully of soft fruits, a perfume which takes Jax right back to a summer of sandpits and sunshine.

'Thanks Katie. Yes, as you can see I'm standing here outside the Barracks Bakery, where the launch party is taking place for *Food of Love*–' (just in time, the girl with sprayed-on trousers has passed him a copy. It is heavier than he expects, so when he holds it up to camera, his wrist bends painfully). 'And with me is the woman who wrote it, who needs no introduction, no surname in fact, she's that famous. The guru of gastronomy—Majella.'

Applause breaks out, apparently spontaneously, until Jax spots the girl in tight trews, whipping it up with all the enthusiasm of a glum seal.

PARTY FOOD

The interviewer turns to face her. 'So, do we really need more cookbooks, Majella?'

Closed question, thinks Jax. Questions that can be answered with a simple yes or no. Bad journalistic training. Although Majella is too experienced not to give the programme what it wants. We have all become performing seals, thinks Jax.

'Not more cookbooks, Freddie, just good ones. Which is why my publishers have reissued mine, the *Food of Love*. It's updated, it's contemporary, but it still remains the best.'

'So, what do you mean by contemporary, Majella?'

'Well, in addition to recipes for various food allergies and intolerances, Freddie, we have recipes from Burma and a whole section on making sushi.'

'Yes. But finally, eating out is so cheap now, restaurants in the capital are booming, defying austerity so we hear. Do we really need to cook?'

Majella needs to cook, thinks Jax. She needs the order and the structure and the performance of it. She needs to be noticed. As if cooking the perfect meal might bring Majella's mother back from the torrid contours of Madrid. Or stop her leaving at all.

Jax gazes up at Majella and waits for the expected fluency, with its touch of humility or condescension, depending on the audience. But instead there's just a gaping silence. It hangs between Freddie and Majella like spittle; Jax can almost see it glittering in the arc lights. She glances at Freddie, whose startled hair is trembling. He is twiddling with his earpiece as if someone in a TV gallery somewhere has started screaming. Silence on live television is the abyss.

HUNGRY FOR LOVE

'You know,' Freddie ad libs loudly, frantically, 'restaurants booming, eating out, et cetera, et cetera, do we really need to cook?'

Jax is close enough to stroke those glowing hairs on Majella's neck. They make her mother seem immensely helpless. And it occurs to Jax that the time has come for her to step in and rescue her mother.

'Well, it's interesting you should say that, Freddie, because here, at the Barracks Bakery,' says Majella, indicating over her shoulder, 'you have a fine example of a sound culinary enterprise, much adored by its clients, serving fabulous, inventive food, run by a passionate man who cares about what he makes, fresh every day, on the premises, and the shocking thing is, it's about to be demolished–'

There's a gasp from the audience. Not orchestrated by the seal.

'Demolished?'

'Yes, Freddie. And frankly if I could donate all the sales from *Food of Love*, of which I hope there will be many, to stop the Barracks Bakery being forcibly purchased, I would. But it wouldn't be enough. Can you believe it? It wouldn't be enough. The price is too high. Some people only put greed before nourishment. And that's why we all need to cook, Freddie, to understand how important it is to nourish ourselves, and nourish the nation. So save the Barracks Bakery.' She delivers this final instruction direct to camera. Like a pro.

As the crowd surges back into the cafe behind Majella and her invisible yet demonstrably proficient pipes, Jax is left wondering about the apparent irony of Majella, with a cookery book to sell, urging people not to cook but to rescue a venue selling baked goods ready-made. Still, she is quite overcome at her mother's unexpected generosity of spirit. Behind her she can hear Freddie signing off, back to Katie in the studio. The arc lights have been turned off and, on the pavement, Jax feels the world has become suddenly very obscure and unpredictable.

FUSION

'…which is where ingredients, herbs, or cooking techniques from different cuisines are blended to create exciting combinations for taste and texture. Being different is not the same as being delicious, but there are some ideas which work well, such as…'

Inside, Sonya and her girls are back on duty. The talk is of rescuing whoever is behind such melt-in-the-mouth confections. Jax finally makes it through the crush to the kitchen to see if she can help plate up, and finds Dan. He is steadily washing up by hand, as if he must do penance for letting down the cafe. Out, out, damn spot.

'Where on earth have you been? I've been looking for you everywhere.'

'Is everything going OK? Is there enough food?' Gloves of suds reach all the way to Dan's elbows.

'Stuff the food. My mother's just appealed on TV for the bakery to be saved.'

'Tell her I'm very grateful,' he sighs, wiping his sudsy hands on his apron.

A waitress breezes in and seizes a platter of blood orange madeleines before sweeping out again. The oranges, technically out of season, Dan had sourced from a Turkish wholesaler in Acton. Attention to detail. Every task he fulfils he fears could be for the last time. And he can't bear that his hopes will soon be dashed. He dries his hands.

'You left this,' he says, reaching into a cupboard. 'I read a bit of it. I hope you don't mind.'

She takes it from him, feeling the recognisable weight of it, the familiar smoothness of the leather in her hands. The

FUSION

handover carries all the solemnity of a goodbye gift, and her heart jolts. It hasn't occurred to her that when the cafe closes, Dan might not remain in her life. 'Dan, are you OK?'

'I kept the feather in it. I thought it might be important.'

She glances down. 'Oh, what, the pigeon feather?'

'Pigeon?'

'Yeah. There's a family of them live in the area outside my flat, under the iron steps. They're moulting like crazy at the moment. Great bookmarks, but probably not very hygienic.' Behind her she can hear the vocal swell of a good party in full swing. 'Come on. Everyone's dying to meet you.' She holds out her hand.

'I can't. I mean–' Though he longs to clasp her hand, he also dreads it. To hold is just a foretaste of to lose. He's afraid to explain that without the cafe he will be nothing, that out of this failure he fears losing her forever. Better abandon the cafe and confront the loss upfront. Now; today. A burst of nausea rolls through him. Only a fool could have mistaken a pigeon moult for an angelic missive. He doesn't know what he believes in anymore, but it sure as hell isn't himself.

Jax has turned to the page with the feather. *Ulysses*. Dan now knows the poem off by heart. 'To strive, to seek, to find, and not to yield'. He had hoped that repetition might bring about some kind of inner transformation. He watches Jax as she reads the poem, her fringe swishing imperceptibly to the rhythm of the text. He feels lost.

Beyond the kitchen door another bottle of champagne is enthusiastically uncorked.

He must keep Jax here for five more minutes, in case they are their last together. 'Why do you read poetry?'

HUNGRY FOR LOVE

'I don't, much,' she says, her finger marking the line she has reached. 'Caryl's the literary one.' She resists telling Dan about Caryl and Toby, in case she jinxes something. 'I turn to this more because my father gave it to me. I find it reassuring. Isn't that why people read poetry? For guidance, comfort?'

'Like people preferring cappuccino cupcakes?'

She loves that he remembers this. His eyes, she sees properly, are the colour of broad beans—the washed green of the husks and a hint of the emerald within. 'Maybe we're all trying to sooth ourselves.' She is thinking of Caryl cutting herself, Majella cooking, Mike and nicotine, Conrad hiding behind cameras. And her, sex with two men in quick succession and a recent addiction to *mise en place*. None of the tactics would seem especially successful, or maybe only partially so. A price is always paid.

I hold myself back, Dan longs to say. I hold myself back when I mean to be open. And what this means is that, when I do open up, I do it jerkily. 'Tennyson apparently lost the love of his life.'

'Yes. Arthur Hallam.'

'I read it in the introduction. I guess writing soothed him.'

'I thought Jonty was the love of my life. And then he betrayed me and I saw that I was mistaken. That really hurt.'

'And when does the pain of losing someone you love end?'

Jax thinks for a moment. 'I think that what happens is not that it ends, but that you rebuild yourself around it.'

'To strive, to seek, to find, and not to yield?'

FUSION

'Something like that,' she says, closing the book firmly shut. It has choked her to hear Desmond's words spoken to her after all these years. She blinks a tear away and glances around the kitchen. The fan-assisted oven purrs over its final batch of tartlets, the mixing bowls are neatly stacked, vanilla and basil perfume the air, the dishwasher hums its cycle, the many cookery books line the shelves, waiting patiently to offer up more secrets. Caryl was right, Jax has experienced happiness in this place. Cooking and friendship, the perfect combination. If only she could stay here and cook. She doesn't want to work at *Your Day* anymore, she loves food, she wants to cook. *Good grief, she wants to cook!* A smile tingles on her lips. She will cook for Dan, and Caryl—hopefully with Toby in tow—for Mike perhaps, to wean him off the Chinese takeaways, and for herself. And she will cook for Majella.

The oven timer starts beeping.

Toby pops his head round the door. 'There you are! There's a man desperate to speak to you. He hasn't got an invite, so they're not letting him in. He's getting antsy. You need to come.'

Jax has an image of Jonty—beery and smelling of dog poo—being obnoxious. How dare he turn up here and cause a scene, tonight of all nights. 'Can't your bouncers get rid of him?'

Toby shrugs. 'We've tried that. But he's insistent. Saw you on telly just now, next to your Mum on the news.'

'It's Jonty, isn't it?'

'Yes.' Toby frowns. 'No, *he* came earlier, but he was so drunk he was easy to get rid of. This one's called Brian.'

Dan, taking the Tennyson from her, urges Jax to go— 'go, the filo will catch if I don't attend to these tarts at once'.

HUNGRY FOR LOVE

But in truth it takes but seconds for a practised hand to whisk a hot tray safely out of the oven. From around the door Dan watches Jax Gay-Gordoning her way through the crowd, stepping further and further out of reach, the gentle sway of her hips vaguely hypnotic. And as he witnesses the moment when she comes face to face with a man at the door dressed in a monogrammed shirt and quilted baseball cap, Dan feels as though he has morphed into Baloo or Bagheera as they stand helpless in the jungle watching Mowgli amble innocently over to the man camp.

CHOCOLATE VELVET CUPCAKES

'…which is a recipe which remains secret to this day. The key to being a good cook is to have a few recipes up your sleeve which you can own: even if you struggle to cook, get to be well known among your friends for your salad dressings, or your dips. Doing one recipe really well is better than making inedible food all the time…'

'Hello, my English rose.' Brian seizes two flutes of champagne from a passing tray and hands her one. They clink glasses.

At the sound of his cantaloupe voice, Jax has a memory of ice cream being licked from her stomach and she shivers. She takes a fortifying gulp of alcohol. 'I have a feeling you've been avoiding me.'

Brian tugs nervously at the peak of his baseball cap. 'Are you cross?'

'A little. But I was going to call you tomorrow, after the party.' She gestures at the room. 'As you can see, it's all been a bit busy round here.'

Brian smiles at the typical English understatement. He wishes he had the knack. He wishes he could tap into that same casual way of speaking, but his heart is too full. He aches for Jax. Years of longing to rescue his mother and the unexpected sight of Jax on his television screen have led him here tonight. Something about the scene he caught on the news, the impassioned speech of the woman in crimson, the gasps from the crowd—he wasn't really concentrating— convinced him he was needed. And that he needs Jax too, to rescue him from a detached life of globetrotting and badly-translated gym class schedules. They need each other.

HUNGRY FOR LOVE

'And Pablo?' she asks, as though sucking a lemon.

'Pablo?'

'Pablo. Is he here?'

'Lord, no. Pablo's back at the apartment, shagging a girl he met on the plane over. She hasn't just come with emotional baggage, she's brought an entire carousel.'

Jax grins. 'But then Pablo's insatiable. He's a chef.'

'Exactly. A chef and the soon-to-be star of my latest TV franchise, *Cooking Uncovered*. A series in twelve parts. Having him stay over in my apartment was the only way I could keep an eye on him until he's signed on the dotted line!'

So they weren't an item. 'So *that's* what you do. I think I still reckoned you worked in insurance.'

Brian longs to say something witty—I can be your life-long insurance policy, will you marry me—but instead takes another mouthful of champagne.

Jax sees in his eyes that he is on the verge of some sort of declaration, or at least she thinks he might be. She can feel the tips of her ears starting to burn. His lips are wet, almost kissable. 'I don't suppose you'd fancy putting up some money to save the bakery from being knocked down, would you? I know it's rude of me to ask, but seeing as how you're here–'

'Oh my Lord, that's exactly why I'm here! Well, one of the reasons, anyway. I saw this woman on the TV making this appeal and you were standing next to her–'

'You want to give some money?'

'I want to buy the whole thing, Jax! The whole bakery. I love this place. And I can just see it in Santa Monica. And Bangkok–' He reaches for her wrist. 'But Jax, it's not just the bakery I want.'

CHOCOLATE VELVET CUPCAKES

The champagne slops in her glass, its bubbles frothing as if in panic. Jax feels his firm pressure on her arm, his conviction. And she is aware that her hands have become clammy. She doesn't want to upset him, this warm man who has served up such delicious pleasure. She knows she needs to let him down, quickly but gently. A relationship based on even the tiniest expectation of gratitude is but a burnt offering.

And there was a time when she was just that—pathetically grateful—that any man should want her after her mother's indifference. It was the mistake she made with Jonty and she nearly made the same mistake when running after Brian.

'I'm so sorry, Brian. It's all my fault. You've made me very happy, and I like you a hell of a lot. But I feel really bad. I shouldn't have flirted with rescue when I had no intention of being saved.'

And as she leans forward to kiss him gently on the cheek, remembering his tongue in her most intimate spaces, she knows none the less that she is doing the right thing.

Brian feels the light touch of her skin against his. He senses her pulling away, like cake from the side of the tin, as if their time is done. He wants to beg her to reconsider, but swallows it; you can't, he realises, force-feed love. He remembers his first visit with Jax to this bakery, noticing the way Dan looked at Jax, couldn't take his eyes off her in fact, even when he was handing out change or wrapping slices of cake in khaki parchment.

'Tell me more about the bakery stuff,' Brian says at last, after a few deep breaths, when he is sure he won't embarrass himself by choking up. 'How much does Dan need?'

HUNGRY FOR LOVE

'Who's Jacqueline talking to?' asks Majella. 'The chap in the baseball cap?'

The launch crowd has thinned out. Sonya's girls are filling bin liners with party debris; Sonya has already carried several bags to the black bin in the next street. Mike followed her, even lit her a cigarette on the way back—for which she was, apparently, gasping. Conrad has sold some snaps to a national diary column and is already at work in his darkroom at home. Toby's team is busy breaking down the cardboard boxes which earlier this evening housed newly-minted copies of *Food of Love*. Every single copy has been sold, despite the relatively stingy discount on the night. Majella is rubbing at the webbing between thumb and forefinger to alleviate author's signing cramp.

'Oh him? That's Brian,' says Caryl. 'He's a trillionnaire.'

'How on earth do you know? Is he one of your patients?'

'Nope. He's a friend of Jax's. A very good friend, I gather. So I googled him. He gave five billion dollars away to charity last year. He owns a TV production company with global franchises.'

'Does he now?'

'Mother. Don't be greedy.'

'What I mean is, are he and my daughter an item?' The question is not an idle one. Does this man possess a kitchen to rival Jonty's, which Majella might one day have access to?

'What is it with mothers, always trying to marry off their daughters?'

'Not that I'll have to try for you, it seems,' says Majella, nodding in the direction of Toby. He is carefully unstringing the pea lights, having commandeered the one chair in the cafe. Caryl gazes at him. His balancing act is impressive. The hefty thread of his jacket feels warm around her shoulders. She crosses her scabbed wrists to draw its lapels closer to her. She hasn't wanted to hide in the bathroom once, tonight.

Brian is finishing a cupcake, licking the icing along with his wounds. He sits unobtrusively in a corner. Despite a healthy bank balance and a career in media, Brian isn't comfortable centre stage.

He wipes his mouth on a napkin. He is watching Jax, who has gone over to break the news to Dan. All his life, Brian has been looking for his damsel in distress and now she turns out to be a man. Rescuing the Barracks Bakery, and Dan's vision about baking, feels fitting: his money and his actions finally facilitating something of permanence. It feels like the right kind of legacy.

Dan is in the kitchen, sitting down. In some cultures, this is the classic remedy for shock.

'He's buying the whole bloody cafe? Are you sure?'

'The whole *building*.'

'Bloody hell, can he?'

'Apparently. He's bidding more than anyone else. And my mother's publicist Toby has a sister who's a property lawyer. She's already looked at the contracts and the one your original developer was using is flawed in some way.'

'The whole building?'

'Yes.'

'I could expand.'

'If you wanted.'

HUNGRY FOR LOVE

Dan's mind is racing. He thinks back to the Tennyson, how he had taken it from Jax when Brian arrived and placed it in the bread barrel, for safe keeping. The feather he had tipped out of shame into the pedal bin. He is regretting that now. Just as he is regretting still wearing his food-splattered apron while Brian sits in the cafe, resplendent in expensive headgear. Dan wonders whether this is significant. Clearly angels come in many guises, not just with white feathered wings as seen in stained glass windows. Evidently some have unusual taste in hats, to go with an American accent.

He is not clear where this new arrangement leaves him and Brian. Like rutting stags, perhaps. Or where it leaves him and Jax. And it occurs to Dan that he might be being bought off, that the cafe is now nothing more than a consolation prize, to clear the way for some transatlantic merger. He hopes to God Jax and Brian don't ask him to make a wedding cake, that really would be the, well, the icing. Ha, no, not the icing. He laughs.

The messiness of life, someone once said, is like the offcuts from the pastry lining the perfect apple pie. In which case, Dan realises, gathering up the trimmings, balling them together, and flouring life's rolling pin again is simply part of any cook's job. 'And not to yield'. Perhaps Tennyson was a closet kitchen bandit.

Jax is now fingering Dan's extensive collection of cookbooks. Majella has a similar hoard at home but Jax has always ignored them, as if they were merely photos of rivals. The awareness of her lack of knowledge, and the dark shape of regret at it, has lately become a shadow in her gut.

CHOCOLATE VELVET CUPCAKES

Dan's books are well used, the spines cracked, the covers grubby. She traces the letters of their titles, breathing deeply. Through her fingertips she can detect the pulse of a world of recipes, of pleasure that awaits. Pablo and Brian showed her that. She can read and she can cook. The air around her vibrates with companionship and nurture and something just a little bit devilish.

She turns round from the cookery books and leans her rump against the kitchen counter. Dan is sitting with a cupcake in his lap, the last of the evening's chocolate velvets. Jax thinks its dome of buttercream looks achingly tempting. Just seeing it there makes her want to sink to her knees and start licking.

He looks up at her, aware suddenly of all he has ever wanted to say, of all he had always hoped his food might slice through to.

'I made this for you,' he says, quietly.

Jax smiles and pushes off from the kitchen counter.

'I think you'll find I made that batch last night,' she smiles. And then she leans towards him—so close that he can smell the vanilla in her shampoo—and scoops up buttercream on a finger. Eyeing him, she brings her finger to her mouth and closes her lips around it. When she pulls it out, the buttercream is gone, leaving a moist tip. She turns and walks out of the kitchen.

Dan watches her leave, her summer dress skimming her elegant curves. Food, he knows, isn't quite the whole story. His heart feels as though it's on a rolling boil.

'Jax.'

In the middle of the room, Jax turns to find Dan standing in the doorway, the cupcake with its lopsided dome still in his hand. Indeed, everyone left in the cafe has turned to stare at the man in the suds-splattered apron. Dan can feel their eyes scalding his skin.

'I made this for you,' says Dan again. But as he glances down at the half-eaten buttercream, he understands why some in the room have started to giggle.

'And like I said,' says Jax patiently, 'I think you'll find I made that particular batch last night.'

Dan's freckles are on fire. He holds out the cupcake to find that his hand is shaking. 'No, what I mean is, I invented this recipe for you. The chocolate velvet, it's you. It's everything I've ever wanted to say about you but could never put into words. It has the softest crumb of all my cakes because you're so tender. And it has the most complex chocolate flavours, but with Ovaltine for some mystery. And a hint of chili for that edge of naughtiness about you which everyone adores. And I sprinkled it with tiny, red sugar hearts, not that it needs it because you're pretty enough on your own. I invented it because I love you. I have always loved you. And I want to spend my life cooking with you. Please, come and cook beside me at my stove?'

'I knew it was chili,' whispers Majella, to no one in particular.

Jax feels something shift inside her, a movement as subtle yet precise as an oven reaching the correct temperature. And in that moment Jax understands how to love. That you can love food, and activities like cooking and sex, but that human love possesses an added ingredient: a kind of stability in two equal partners, with added chili. She walks up to Dan, takes his face in her hands and kisses him firmly on the lips.

CHOCOLATE VELVET CUPCAKES

Dan leans into the warmth of her, drinking in the sweetness of her mouth, his senses alive with the taste of a life rather than an existence. It is, he realises, the most complete flavour he has ever tasted.

LEFTOVERS

'…which is funny, because this is my favourite aspect of cooking—
using up what's left over. I am at my most inspired when I have little
things to work with, things the thrifty part of me can't bear to see
thrown away. So whether it's rissoles, risotto, a quiche or a trifle, it's
time to celebrate the scraps and…'

The evening light is deepening to mauve. The last few
guests are wending their way home. The air vibrates with
the news that Dan and Jax are soon to occupy adjoining
stoves. She is, she has announced to the room, resigning
from *Your Day* and apprenticing herself to the Barracks
Bakery. Desmond—and his mate, Tennyson, possibly—
would approve.

Brian has been chatting to Majella while admiring the
Thanksgiving proportions of her cleavage. It occurs to him
that what Pablo's show might need in order to capture the
crucial West Coast daytime audience is a mother figure foil.
He will put in a call to L.A tomorrow. Hell—maybe he,
like, needs a mother figure too.

Toby walks Caryl back to Jax's flat. As he passes one of
the council's black rubbish bins he drops a crumpled envelope into its greedy mouth.

Mike, when Jax finds him outside in a clinch with Sonya,
refuses her resignation, but demands instead, on *Your Day*'s
behalf, first dibs on the wedding coverage, for which he
earns a playful slap. Failing that, he says, you can start writing a beginner's cookery column, instructing new brides.
Getting the recipes wrong so *Your Day*'s readers don't have
to. That earns him his second slap.

LEFTOVERS

As she and Dan lock up together, Jax can't help smiling at this evening's developments. Food isn't just love, it embraces a whole way of being. Having once rejected the homely realm of domestic science, she is now keen to reclaim it. From the moment Majella made her televised rescue appeal, a gesture not for herself but for someone else, Jax has felt as though a place has finally been set for her at her mother's table. Anything, Jax knows now, is possible.

Majella is on the last train as it pulls out of Victoria. A conductor electronically scans her flimsy ticket. It's an unnecessarily wordless exchange—a symptom, Majella feels, of a world fraught with loosened connections.

She stares out the window, into other people's kitchens. My daughter wants to cook. Not be a cook, necessarily, but to cook for a while at the bakery, until she is ready to make more formal plans. Pulling back slightly Majella can see her own reflection as the twilit suburbs hurtle by. In the corner of her eye glints a salty bead of water. She blows her nose.

Something rams into the back of her seat.

'Sorry, madam.'

She twists round and looks up. A pimpled man in a lurid corporate tie is struggling to manoeuvre the buffet cart as they race through Earlsfield.

'Refreshments?' The man privately reflects on the decline of impulse buying today. He blames the spate of makeover shows and celebrities with cellulite, especially the men.

Back home, where Parkin waits with a certain complacent hauteur for reports from the front, there is leftover cassoulet in the fridge, pre-sliced brioche in the freezer, and some ripe mango for a fool. There's half a cup of fennel soup, a bunch of watercress and a few cubes of syrupy baklava. Or there are rice noodles in the cupboard, next to the chili jam which sets off the reblochon currently stinking out the larder. The celery seed biscuits she made last week would go well with that. Nothing will take too much time to prepare or assemble.

'What have you got?' she asks.

He rattles through the options, with little hope.

Majella thinks back to the cassoulet. Next time she must remember to use less thyme, it's too woody at this time of year. Playing with food, it's what she does. And yet right now, Majella isn't sure she can be bothered. She has had such a lovely, lovely evening, being nice to people. The book, yes. And Caryl's new beau. But Jacqueline is going to be a *cook*.

'I'll take the cheese and pickle, please.'

'White or brown?'

'White. And one of those cans of drink.'

The man hands Majella her change, and then steers his cart along the empty corridor before disappearing through sliding doors.

Majella unfolds her tissue napkin and spreads it on the table jutting out from the wall, with all the care of someone laying a special picnic. She then peels back the film on the plastic pyramid and removes the sandwiches. The tang of commercial chutney tickles her nose. The train is cruising through fields now, with all the lilt of a lullaby. She picks up one flabby triangle—it droops a little in her hand— and carefully tears it in half to make two smaller ones.

LEFTOVERS

She does the same with the other sandwich, until she has four. She smiles when she sees what she has done. Majella's mother always used to cut up her little girl's sandwiches into quarters.

ACKNOWLEDGEMENTS

A writer's life is nourished in many, unrelated-to-writing ways, so my grateful thanks go to:

Shomit Mitter, for inspired *mise en place;*
My mother, for raspberry cheesecake, Possum Pie and that Chinese restaurant in Bognor Regis;
Virginia Whetter, for soups and solace;
Anne-Marie Williams, for Rose Levy Beranbaum and her Golden Almond Cake;
Jax Meikle, for her name, her chutney and her ability to 'make a plan';
The Wimpole Street Writers, for early nudges, and the RFH writing group for timely seasoning and cashew nuts;
Jeremy Sheldon, for good milk at just the right time;
Michael Arditti, for wise counsel and ginger oatcakes;
Toby Parsons, for military rations;
Grace Dugdale for chips and mayo, Hannah Vaughan Jones for Spirulina and Sasha Waddell for many evenings in Carluccio's;
The wonderful team at Quartet, Naim Attallah, Gavin James Bower, Anna Stothard, Grace Pilkington, Vicky Scott and Nici West, for the icing on the cake;
And above all to Guy, for Love Salad, brockley (sic) and being the Johnny to my Fanny.

Because, as the great man once said (Nigel Slater, *Appetite*):

> "If you do decide to go through life without cooking…
> you are losing out on one of the greatest pleasures
> you can have with your clothes on."